Genre-fluid

Gabriel Oakthorn

Published by Lucid Tales, 2020.

GENRE-FLUID

First edition. November 27, 2020.

ISBN: 979-8227811660

Written by Gabriel Oakthorn.

Table of Contents

For my wonderful grandmothers.

Thank you for all your encouragement, you mean
the world to me.

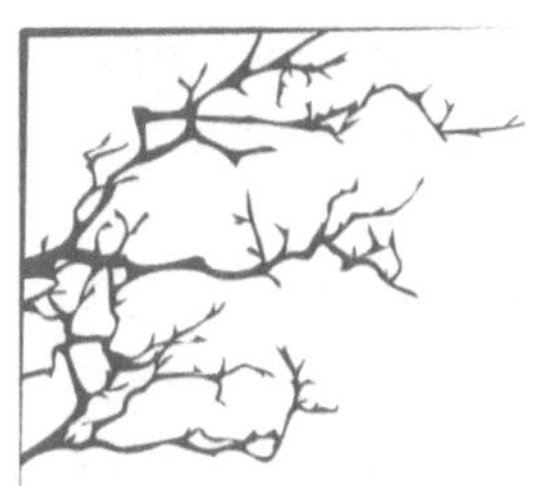

The Frost

THE NIGHTS WERE DRAWING in, and the Frost was starting to touch the land again. Maria pulled her cloak tighter around her and quickened her pace toward home. She passed no one on the moor-road. Most people were sensible enough not to risk getting caught out after dark.

The sun was steadily slipping below the horizon and her breath was misting in the cold air. She broke into a jog, hitching her heavy skirts up around her ankles. As the final sliver of sun slipped below the land, she saw the welcome light of her doorway, the beloved shadow of her husband standing looking out. The light was fading faster now that the sun was gone, and the chill was biting at her thin, bare fingers.

She slowed as she reached the gate outside the cottage, and let herself in. The cold iron bit into her skin and she hurried through, closing it carefully and running up the path to the front door.

Her husband, Tae, stepped aside as she entered, and closed the door before catching her up in a tight hug, kissing her cold face. In contrast, his heat felt burning. She smiled into his kiss and relaxed into the warmth of his embrace.

'Cutting it fine, love,' he chastised gently.

Maria turned away to pull in the latch-string for the night. 'A necessary evil. At least I have them now.'

'You found them?' Tae's eyes widened. He grinned suddenly. 'Should have known you'd manage it, even at this time of year.'

'Doubting me already, husband of mine?' Maria teased, taking his hand and heading to the table. The room wasn't yet much warmer than outside; the fire had been untended too long. 'It's colder than a witch's nipple in here, Tae.'

'Sorry, love. Waiting for you to outrun Frost gets a bit tense.' He crossed to the fireplace and gently coaxed the fire back into being. Maria moved to sit beside him, stretching her tawny, frozen hands out to the flames.

'You sure you don't want to just sit in the damn fire?'
Tae laughed.

'Burned enough witches around here, thank you very much.' Maria gave him a friendly shove.

'Careful, I'll be for dinner next if you push me in the fire again.'

'What *is* for dinner?'

'Have a guess.'

Maria sighed. 'Stew.' Like every other night since winter returned.

Tae smiled wryly. 'You win. Unfortunately, the prize is also stew.'

'Exciting.' Maria pushed herself to a standing position and brushed the dirt off her knees. 'Did you add much to it or just keep stirring?'

'I pulled up some of the Frost-bitten carrots and radishes and put them in.'

'Radishes? In stew?' Maria wrinkled her nose.

'At least this way we can eat them rather than wasting them for poisoned.' Tae stood and lifted the lid of the pot above the fire. Quickly poking a finger in, he tasted the stew inside. 'Lukewarm. Sorry, Mari. It'll heat up soon enough.'

She pulled her shawl closer. 'Ah well. It gives us some time to prepare the herbs. Get us a knife.'

Half an hour later, Tae got up to check on the stew, his hands red with the juice from the shredded bloodthorn. Maria swept the slender tendrils off the table and into a small earthenware jar. Securing the lid, she placed the jar on the mantel above the fireplace, beside a row of similar pots.

'It's done, I think,' Tae said, swinging the pot out from over the fire.

'All right. Go wash your hands and I'll clean up the table.'

Tae glanced out of the window. 'Frost is in full force.' Shaking his head with a sigh, he soaked his hands in the washing bowl beside their rough bed. Maria scrubbed the table with soapsand and water, trying to get the last stains of the bloodthorn juice out of the grain. It was never a good idea to have the sap around too long – it was a bad-luck plant, bringer of death and poisons.

Outside, the Frost crept, curling around the houses, staring in at windows and painting them with its icy breath, jealous of the heat within. It slipped through the valleys and coated the hills, covering the land in a pale sheet, freezing blades of grass and sheathing ponds in ice, creating a frozen landscape in which it was king.

By morning, the house was cold. Maria woke and at first wriggled closer to Tae, to warm herself. Then, realising the fire was out, she sighed and opened her eyes to the cold, grey light of dawn. She reached for her shawl and sat up, pulling it around her shoulders. It was far too cold to be awake at this hour, and the witchblood was burning this morning, racing through her veins like full-body heartburn.

Groaning, she placed her feet on the frozen, packed-earth ground with its thin covering of rushes, and resigned herself to chilblains. She stood and shuffled over to the still-warm grate and began building a small cooking fire. It was never a good idea to let a fire burn out now that Frost had returned. The thought of the Frost set her blood burning hotter and she nearly went straight for the earthenware jars, but restrained herself. *Later,* she reminded herself. It wouldn't do to waste the contents on an impulse.

She struck sparks onto the dried leaves and kindling, but they steadfastly refused to take, cold through like she was. She muttered a curse under her breath and looked over to where Tae was still quietly snoring. He always was a heavy sleeper. She quickly snapped her fingers and made a sharp gesture. Fire leapt in the grate, sending the leaves and twigs merrily crackling. Within a few minutes, one of the logs had caught, and Maria stood to return to bed for a while longer. She didn't have to be up before sunrise now, after their cow, Slip, got Frost-bitten. A sad convenience. Maria missed her.

'Mari?' Tae's sleepy voice startled her and she smiled.

'I'm here, love. I was just relighting the fire.'

'Come back to bed, dearheart.'

Maria slid back under the rough woollen blanket and pressed close against Tae.

He rolled to look at her and frowned. 'You promised, Mari. It's too dangerous to use it lightly like that. What if a hunter hears and comes for you?'

Maria didn't reply, a wave of distant guilt drifting through her. There was silence for a moment.

'How can you tell?' she asked quietly.

'Your eyes are always so bright afterwards,' Tae murmured, stroking her cheek.

'I can't help it. I'm made for it. Sometimes it just slips out.'

'I know, love, I know.' He pulled her close and stroked her hair. Usually the gesture would have calmed her, but this morning her blood was burning and she pulled away.

'I think it's tonight.' She left the bed again, ignoring the cold floor on her feet. She crossed to the window and breathed on it, clearing a small circle of Frost-feathers. When she was a little girl, she'd loved playing with them. Now they were a symbol of everything she had come to hate.

'Tonight?' Tae sat up and scrambled to his feet, pulling the blanket around his broad shoulders. 'Are you sure, Mari? It's not yet the solstice.'

The world outside was cold and silent, frozen to the bone. The grass was white, the vegetables Frost-bitten. Any animals out last night would now be solid, staring lumps of ice. She clenched her teeth.

'Tonight. I can feel it burning. It's calling me, Tae.' The Frost was not an adversary to be taken lightly, and the solstice would be when she was at her most powerful, but the singing in her bones told her that by then it would be too late.

'I don't think it's a good idea, Maria.'

She sighed and leaned her forehead against the glass. She loved her husband dearly, but he was not a witch. There was not one drop of witchblood in him, let alone the instincts that came with it. They operated on entirely different planes.

'There is no other way. It must be tonight.'

'Love, you need-'

She felt his hands reaching out to touch her shoulders.

'Don't tell me what I need, Tae,' she snapped, turning to face him. The hurt in his face halted her and she sighed, softening. 'I trust you to know best how to butcher a cow, plough a field and turn wood into beauty. You must trust me when I say this, Tae. It must happen tonight.'

Tae's blue eyes bored into hers, doubt and love and worry filling them. 'I trust you.'

That afternoon, once the sun was shining and the frost melted away, they made their way up to the Ring. The Ring was an ancient circle from before the first Frost, many centuries before. Formed of three rings, two stone and one earth, it was full of old power, soaked into the very rocks. It was on the crest of Devil's Hill, and once witches were believed to copulate with the Devil there to create changelings and body-born demons. Most people didn't believe that now; witches were either disbelieved or ignored for the most part. Unless the hunters came to town, but they never bothered with small villages like this, with their smattering of houses and not even a market.

Maria finished the climb just ahead of Tae and set down her bundle in the centre of the rings of stone and earth. She went to one of the towering pillars of rock and reverently stroked a hand down it, feeling the power deep within. Tae dropped his bundle beside hers and stood behind her, sliding his arms around her waist and looking at the view over her shoulder. For a moment, she let herself relax into him, imagining that the country laid out so beautifully before her was free of the blight of the Frost, that the evil that crept in the darkness was banished once more.

But that was not the case, and the world got colder every year. She shook herself and stepped away from Tae. There was much to do before sundown.

Maria spent the rest of the afternoon directing Tae to tie bundles of herbs into different pouches, and hang them from the highest tops of the stones. She herself buried bloodthorn and dark-knot at the foot of the outermost circle, gorberry and leonand in the earthen bank, and earthblood, snowberry and bowranth under the innermost circle of stones. Banishment and bad luck, protection and good luck, power and warmth. When at last she had finished, she stood in the centre of the circle and spread her arms, stretching out her fingers as she cast out her power, feeling it radiate within the circles, made stronger by the herbs. Pulling herself back in, she nodded in satisfaction.

'I'm all done, love. Where do you want me?' Tae hugged her briefly.

She turned away. 'At home. Where it's safe.'

He opened his mouth to protest.

'The battle tonight will not be easily won, Tae, and I cannot protect you as well as myself. At home you will be safe.'

'I want to be able to protect you if I have to,' he said stubbornly.

'You can't. This is a battle of witches, love. A mortal man has no place here.' She held him tight to her. 'Only one can leave the circle alive once it has been fully cast. I don't want to lose you even if I myself must be lost. The land will need you if I am gone.'

'Is there nothing I can do? I can fight, you know that.' Poor, stubborn Tae. He was so dear to her.

'Please go, my love. If you stay, you will die. I could not bear that. Please go. You must be home before dark.'

'And you?'

'I will be safe in the circle until it comes.' If all went according to plan, at least.

Tae's shoulders tensed, but Maria knew he had given in. 'I will keep the candles burning all night for you.'

'I know,' she said. 'I love you.' She held him tighter and kissed him fiercely. 'Please go. Be safe, my love.' She released him and pushed him back a step.

'I will. I love you too, my dearheart. If you are not back by morning, I will come here, Frost or no Frost, and find you.' With that, he left, looking back over his shoulder a few times. Maria watched his solitary figure grow smaller and more distant until he rounded the hill by the village, just as the sun was creeping onto the horizon.

Within a half hour, the sun had set. Maria sat on the cold, hard ground, holding her shawl tight around her shoulders. The air inside the circle was unnaturally warm, even for a night before the Frost had begun creeping in the night. How had it started? Was it a spell someone cast or something more elemental? She had never known, but it had ceased to matter. Whatever it was, however it came about, something must be done.

She pulled her shawl around her shoulders as the grass around the edges of the outer circle began to turn white and stiffen.

A cold breath gusted through the circle and the outer grass began to crumple and blacken, Frost-bitten. It did not fully freeze, however. The outer circle, at least, was strong. Maria scrambled to her feet and firmly dug them into the earth in the very centre of the circles. It was coming.

For almost an hour, she could feel it drawing closer, stealthy and quiet, almost like a living creature. It prowled around the circle, testing her defences, nosing first here then there in search of an opening. Then, suddenly and without warning, it struck.

A howling gale nearly blew Maria off her feet, the icy wind biting right through her. Digging her feet even harder into the ground, she leaned into the force and defied it. She drew her power about her like a cloak, and the gale immediately separated around the warm sphere of energy. Within a second, it dropped. The Frost went back to prowling, more wary now she had shown her power. It howled at her, the chilling sound of a thousand cracking ice rivers, a hundred snow-broken trees falling, a thousand angry winds. She felt a chill in her bones, forcing them to still, dulling the singing, slowly turning her to ice. With a contemptuous flick of her wrist, the ice forming around her shattered, and her bones heated to a searing pain, driving out the Frost.

After that, it began to attack relentlessly, sending shard after shard, icy blasts and cold snows, biting hail and slick ice to batter her, trying to make her lose her footing. She melted any ice around her feet and soon the firm ground was a puddle of muddy slush that seeped into her shoes and bit like teeth. The winds she deflected with her heart's warmth, the snow and hail she melted or bounced off, countering every attack with ease. She began to feel almost confident. Then the Frost reminded her it was no mere witch, no insignificant living creature that could be tricked into submission. It unleashed an absolute stillness. It was the silence of the grave, the coldness of the last light in a man's life, the blindest dark, cloud-covered night, the taste of death and nothingness. The heart of winter. Maria's breath caught, fear and cold in her chest.

This was no spell. No human creature could have cast this, summoned up such a monstrous force. This was something much older and deeper. This was the true power of the Frost. The unending silence of death, the skeletons of trees and the freezing, heartstopping cold of fear. It was this that she would have to do battle with. And she didn't think she could face it.

As she stood there, frost and ice forming on her skin, her boots; her eyelashes freezing solid, she hesitated. And the Frost, sensing her indecision, her weakness, intensified its power. She could feel her hair solidifying, her skin cracking and the blood below freezing before it could even begin to ooze. All was lost. She could no longer move. A wave of despair crashed through her, followed by another. The Frost was winning, holding her in its grip, ready to crush her at any moment. What could she do? She, a mere witchwoman, against the might of true winter. There was nothing. The land would be shrouded in cold for the rest of eternity.

Then a spark lit in her sluggish, frozen mind. A tiny image, a memory. She and Tae, laughing, running home ahead of Frost and slamming the door as the ice crept right up to it. Collapsing in front of the fire together, making love, adrenaline coursing through them, relieved and laughing and *alive*. A warmth returned to her fingers, then crept slowly up her arms, toward her shoulders. Her heart began to beat faster as the heat entered, spreading through her chest and belly. It was like being slipped into a hot bath, pressing against Tae's warm body on a cold morning, stretching her hands out to a fire after a day's work. She would live. They would live. The land would live.

'We beat you then, we can beat you now!' she cried, unleashing her will, her rage and love and fear, spreading it through the circles, lighting on herb pouch after herb pouch, weaving a net of witchery and strength through which the Frost could not hope to escape. The stones lent her their power, strengthening the bonds and pulling the net tight. The Frost gave up its crushing stillness and threw winds, gales, howling blizzards, snow, storms, thunder and lightning, hail and winter rain, ice and death at her, each caught and trapped by the web of power. She spread her fingers wide and clenched them tightly, drawing in the net around the Frost and pulling it down, deep into the ground, right through the centre of the circle and under it. She sent it down into the melting blood of the earth, to the molten, crashing rock and further still. And there she trapped it, speaking the three words of power that no man spoke and lived, binding it beyond any chance of escape. A last, echoing howl issued from the ground, and then all was still.

The night was still cold, but the stars were shining brightly. A flicker of movement; an owl flew overhead. The grass, though it was blackened, was not frozen. The Frost was defeated. Maria caught sight of a rabbit running past and smiled, weary and glad. An omen. The animals would return, already were returning. The land would heal. She stepped out of the puddle around her feet and stared at her badly frostbitten hands. A finger or two in exchange for the land was nothing.

Wearily, she kissed the stone nearest and murmured her gratitude, before facing east and slowly heading toward home.

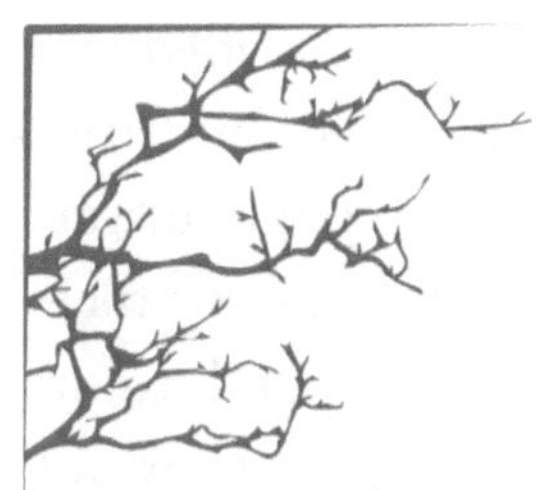

Molly

DATES ARE DIFFICULT. I find it hard to be specific about the earlier centuries of my life; the brain can only hold so many memories, the years blur into one another. I remember that a Caesar was in power in Rome, but beyond that I cannot tell you. In truth, I do not even remember where I was from. It may not even exist anymore.

Once I was one of many, a mortal human, with a set lifespan and no more, but when I was the age I appear to be now – around twenty or so, wouldn't you say? – I was changed. It didn't happen overnight, but gradually. The change wasn't so noticeable at first – at that old, you don't age so fast, and it was normal, then, to be often ignored in favour of those who were older, more experienced, wiser, men. And then, of course, I entered that period of self-important study that it seems all young people go through, posturing and sitting alone in my rooms, reading Aristotle and Socrates by candlelight, pretentious to a fault. At that point, I hardly noticed that no one was talking to me, I was so busy talking to *them*. And if they didn't seem to be listening, that was fine too; I was more than enough entertainer and audience to appreciate my own genius. I have a vague notion now that they didn't approve. Wherever I was, their perceptions of women and education seemed positively patriarchal. What else has not changed?

However, my blithe insensitivity to my peers faded with time, and I realised that perhaps I had alienated my friends during that period, been just a little too self-congratulatory, and began attempting to make amends with some of them. I couldn't understand why they did not respond to my invitations, nor why it was so difficult persuading my servants to bring me food on occasion. Only after I had gone three weeks without it did I realise that it had become unnecessary. After that, I began to pay attention.

I noticed that it wasn't simply my friends who were ignoring me, but everyone. My servants had continued keeping the place clean and tidy as though waiting for a master to return, and they responded sluggishly to my commands, if they noticed my loud, demanding voice in the first place. As with all young people, being ignored was aggravating and I began to make rather a fool of myself. I would run into the street and flourish a sword at passersby, just to make them notice me. It astounded me that they had no reaction to an edged weapon being waved in their faces until I had continued raving at them long enough, upon which they would give me a vague, queer look, as though I was merely handing out pamphlets. As soon as I paused for breath, their eyes would slide off me and they would walk on past.

After the initial annoyance had passed, I began to find this phenomenon rather amusing, and I admit I took advantage of it many times. It is very easy to steal a pitcher of wine here or a pouch of gold there when no one knows you exist. I even once sneaked into the emperor's or prince's or king's rooms and- well, that's not exactly fit for retelling. Suffice to say, I got up to all the mischief my new little trick could allow me.

And for a while, that was enough. I evaded ill-meaning men with ease, I took whatever I wanted from wherever I wanted it, I hid in baths, etcetera. But very quickly, that all became rather tiresome. I was bored, and I was lonely. I fell madly in love with a girl I saw in the baths, and pursued her relentlessly, as all hotheaded morons do at first. It did me no good, though I doubt the outcome would have been any different had my little problem not arisen. She could neither initiate conversation with me nor remember me long enough for even the briefest of partings. I was as a face one has seen in a crowd a few times; nondescript, insignificant and completely immemorable. Of course, at the time this rent my heart. I tried to kill myself several times, often in front of her, and her absolute indifference cut me deeper than any knife could. Most often I tried to hang myself. But I never had the stamina for it in the end, and so here I am. I still do not quite know whether I am immortal or just exceptionally long-lived.

And so I lived on, down through the long centuries. The biggest advantage of my situation, I've found, is travel; I never have to pay a fare or even really care about where I'm going. I will survive whatever comes my way with ease. I never stay anywhere long enough to fall in love. I learned that the hard way, after so many hundreds of failed romances. Of course, as you can see, my attitude toward that has changed somewhat.

I like America. I have lived here for many decades. I used to come and visit quite regularly before it was 'discovered' as the Europeans insist on calling it even though we all know that, embarrassingly, the Egyptians got here first. Regardless, once I'd realised I couldn't kill myself, I set out to find out what was at the edge of the world. As it turned out, another land, sparsely populated and beautiful and only a few weeks away. Huge. I lived here for about a century almost completely alone, far from the myriad peoples spread across the landscape.

Of course, I continued on my way after crossing northern America – I didn't discover South America for quite some time after that – and eventually reached what I believe is now a part of China. I can't remember if it was then. But there were many beautiful places and people, and I stayed there for a long time too.

Eventually I moved on and found India. I loved India. It was beautiful, it was hot, and the world was bursting with beauty. The air smelt of dust and sun, dirty barefoot children, ripe fruit and above all warmth.

But when colonialism hit, everything changed. I have to admit I left. I couldn't stand watching somewhere I loved so much forced under the thumb of imperialism. I have not been back since.

Despite all the wonderful places I've seen, I still love America the most. It is my home. I hate what has been done to its rolling hills and endless plains, its beautiful people and cultures, its dense forests and silhouetted mountain peaks, but it is the place I choose to be. And now, as you can see, there is another reason.

I said there was another reason why I stay here, and there is. In fact, she is probably the only reason. If I had not met her, I would have left again, disgusted by what has become of this once paradisiacal land. Perhaps I would have sought out the Antarctic, and howled along with the wind for a few centuries. Sometimes it is tiring to always sing alone.

When I said that relationships have been impossible, it had held true for the past two millennia. Recently, very recently, only about twenty years ago, I met the woman I love. She was the same as everyone at first; she didn't see me, or really hear me, but I persisted. I have not persisted for a long time. It has been too painful. But masochism must have been strong in me that day, for persist I did. I followed her to her car from the bar in which she had been sitting, slightly in front of the man I knew meant her harm. When she shifted the keys from between her fingers to unlock the car, he struck. Or he would have done. Needless to say, I intervened. As I recall, he screamed rater satisfyingly when I broke his fingers. He staggered back, looking distraught and howling in pain like some enormous infant. She threw the door of her car open, jumped in, started the engine, and, door still open, reversed into him. Not very hard, more's the pity – it's difficult to get up speed in a multi-storey parking lot – but he got the message and fell over before half-staggering, half-running away. She opened the passenger side door and in no uncertain terms ordered me to get in. I was shocked, and didn't respond at first.

'Get in,' she insisted, scowling at me. I had never heard more beautiful poetry. I complied, and we drove to a nearby late-night diner, where, under the baleful eye of the night barman, we drank bitter coffee together.

'Who are you?' she demanded, 'Why were you following me?'

I must say I floundered. I had not spoken to anyone but myself for well over five hundred years. I cleared my throat, my voice rusty from lack of use,

'I am…' I realised that, so little had it been used, I had all but forgotten my own name. 'I can't remember.' It seemed so silly, then, so utterly apt that the last person of all to forget me was myself, that I burst out laughing. She just watched me with a careful frown, her sooty eyeliner vague and blurry around her eyes. I think she thought I was mad, or drunk, or some combination of the two. At any rate, I'm sure she was questioning the wisdom of her decision to invite me along. I briefly wondered what I looked like. Mirrors had been alien to me for many years. 'I'm sorry.' I tried again. 'I am…' A chance to reinvent myself, perhaps? I took the first name that came into my head. 'Taran. I'm Taran.'

'Did you just make that up on the spot?'

'Yes,' I admitted. 'It's been so long since someone said my name that I have forgotten it.'

'Shit…'

'I followed you because he was following you. It's sometimes useful, not being noticed.' I think she caught the bitter tone in my voice then, because she asked me what I meant. I studied her carefully before deciding to throw all caution to the winds and respond with exactly what I had not intended to: the truth. 'I'm over two thousand years old. I can't kill myself and usually no one can see me.'

The alarm in her eyes indicated that that had probably not been sensible, but as I'd already jumped in up to my neck, I thought I might as well hold my head under the water.

'Watch,' I told her, and stood, keeping my eyes on her. I was afraid, in truth, that if I looked away, she would instantly forget me again. I walked calmly over to the night barkeep and removed his hat. His eyes didn't even flicker. I walked back to her holding it, and handed it to her. She turned it around in her hands and the barman frowned, heading over.

'Very funny, give it back.'

She gave it to him with an apologetic smile, and he returned to his bar with it. Her luminous eyes turned back to me, amazed. Another jolt of shock hit me; she had looked away, interacted with another person, and still she had seen me.

We talked for a long while that night. Well, I did. A few centuries with no one to talk to and you find yourself with quite the flood of words built up. I cried too, and she held me. We agreed to meet the next morning for coffee and with a hopeful, heavy heart, I watched her drive away.

The next morning, I waited for fifteen minutes before walking away. She had forgotten me. Once again, I was alone. Then I saw her hurrying along the pavement towards the coffee shop and the lead weight in my heart lifted, leaving me light enough to run in after her. She sat down, looking around as though confused. I ordered my coffee and carefully watched her for a few minutes. Her eyes slid over me with a frown. She didn't know me. But she had still come. I decided to sit down with her and see what happened, steeling myself to be looked through.

'Is this seat taken?' I asked.

She glanced at me without recognition and shook her head. 'Go right ahead.' She smiled.

'Are you waiting for someone?' I asked, and her forehead creased, a worried frown etched on her pale face. She looked so different from the night before, her skin bare of its party paint. I could have written poetry about the pores of her skin, her short eyelashes, the dimple in her chin.

'I think so. I said I'd meet someone here, but I can't remember who.' She giggled nervously, looking away and rubbing her forehead. 'I must sound daft.'

'I don't think you're daft,' I said softly. This was strange, new. How could she remember me and yet not remember me? A memory slid through me, fluid and elusive as an eel. This had happened before, at the beginning. I had agreed to meet a friend, and he had arrived but forgotten why. A fragile hope began to build in my chest: maybe it was reversing. Maybe this was a symptom of the fade of my curse – maybe I would be free. The hope was as thin and delicate as an eggshell, and I tucked it away. I didn't want to look at it too closely or it might disappear.

The woman – I realised abruptly I still didn't know her name – was watching me closely with a frown.

'Do I know you?' she asked, eyes narrowing into slits as she struggled to remember. Her knuckles rubbed her forehead until it was red and I wanted to snatch her wrists away, to stop her hurting herself. The translucent skin of her temples looked obscenely vulnerable. I waited, terrified of scaring her away if I told her the truth again.

'I do know you,' she murmured slowly. 'It's like wading through syrup. I met you. You helped me and we had coffee. Did I arrange to meet you here?'

'Yes,' I said quietly, gazing at her. She was beautiful, even with her forehead rubbed red and patchy. In the depths of each tiny flaw there was perfection. 'We met last night.'

"Of course!" She snapped her fingers, suddenly brightening. 'You're the woman from the carpark. You helped me and I drove us to a diner and everyone forgets you and *I just forgot you.*' She looked shocked, staring hard at me with her wide eyes. 'Is that how it happens? Will I just forget you every time you walk away?'

'I don't know,' I murmured, looking at my coffee. 'No one has even seen me for-'

'Two thousand years,' she finished for me, looking awed. 'I remember. I'm sorry. I'm so sorry.'

'What for?' I was puzzled.

'I just *forgot* you.'

I threw my head back and laughed. 'You have nothing to apologise for. Thank you. You're the first person to have seen me in... Thank you.' I didn't cry, this time, but I came close. I had long since lost any embarrassment about such things. When no one can see you, you can cry in public all you like. Her eyes sparkled in the morning light more softly than they had in the harsh light of the diner. I could have forgotten myself, looking into them.

To cut a long story short, we slept together that night. When we awoke, she didn't remember me; thought she must have been out late and picked me up whilst drunk. She was politely friendly but distant, and it took her an hour before she remembered where she knew me from. She laughed and cried, and I cried, but we held each other and got through it. I have lost count now of how many times that has happened.

Some days, she worries it is her, that she has amnesia, that there is something in her head that makes me ineffable, impossible to remember, that she has cancer, dementia, something missing inside. She worries that she is insane, that I am a product of her lonely imagination. On those days my heart aches like her small fist is clenched tight around it and spasming with her sobs. On those days, I am tempted to leave and never come back, to let her forget me and wonder briefly why she spent so many years alone. But I am selfish: I need her. I have spent so many lifetimes alone, entirely separate from the rest of mankind. She is my gift from the gods, my salvation. She *is* my deity. Even that would not be enough to make me stay in the face of her piercing sorrow, but she has made me promise every day since we met that I will not do it, that I will not leave her alone and wondering, will not let me remove my entire presence from her life. When she says this, no matter how many times she has said it before, she is fierce and loyal and full of fire, like a living flame. I would burn down the gates of heaven rather than break my word to her.

After a few weeks together, she took to taking photographs of us together and pinning them everywhere in the flat. Now, so many years on, it looks like a stalker's bedroom from a murder mystery – there is not one space on the walls empty of my face and hers, tired, haggard, laughing, full of love and joy or pain and anger. Even when we fight, she photographs us and keeps it. She says she wants to document us, to force herself to remember me even if I leave and set her free. She says she will use it to find me again. I am undeserving of such unswerving loyalty. I love her with the force of a thousand suns, all the loves and losses of my long life laid out and preserved in her.

But she is getting older. I know it, I see it in her face and her eyes, hear it in her voice, growing husky. She was only twenty two when we met. It has been twenty years since then. For the first time in two millennia I have had to start counting years again. It is exhilarating and terrifying. She will wither and fade, one day, and I will sit by her grave for an eternity. I no longer believe in gods. But I believe in her, and her grave shall be the altar of my worship. I thought I was mad, for a time, but her endless patience, her gentle reminders to her friends, to her family that no, I am not a new lover, they have known me for a long time, they remind me it is churlish to think so.

But I may still go mad, when she finally slips into endless sleep. I remind myself that will not be for at least another forty years. It cannot be. And forty years is a long time when you are paying enough attention to count them. And who knows? I am starting to show signs of growing older myself. The slightest crow feet at the edges of my smile, the first time she looked at me and declared, 'You need a haircut.'

It is slow, but I notice my hair growing again; it never really changes when you're frozen in time. It is not much, but it is a start. Maybe by the time she is ready to die, I will be allowed to follow her. But I doubt it. She is beautiful and wonderful, effervescent and fragile as a butterfly. She will be taken, and I will live on. But now, perhaps, there is an end in sight. I know it worries her too, that she will die and I will be alone. Her eyes are older than her years, she is wise and gorgeously so. She does not speak of it, does not ask, 'when I am dead, will you visit me?'

She does not need to.

But until that day, I will hold her hand as tightly as she holds mine, and I will give thanks every day for her life and her health, her love. She is my angel, my salvation. My Molly.

24

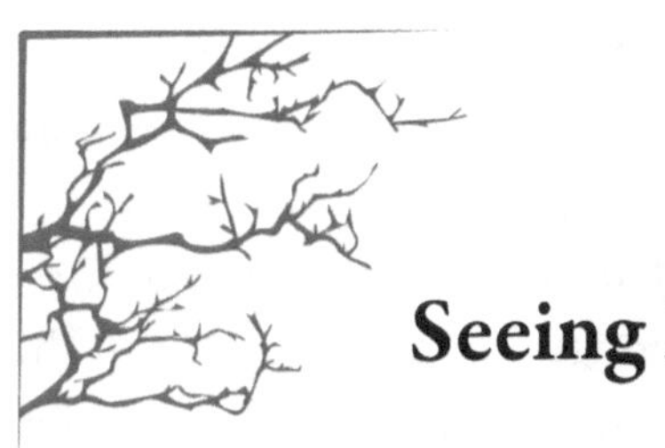

Seeing Double

I SAW MYSELF ON THE subway today. As the train rattled to a stop in the dark between stations, waiting for another tube of commuters to pass us by, something made me look up and out into the blackness over the empty seat opposite. In the curved window I caught sight of my reflection, sallow under the stark lights, with deep purple rings thrown into sharp relief under my eyes. The dank, recycled air had flattened my blonde hair to my head, and given it a frizzy halo around the edges. No makeup, no coffee, after a long day at work. I examined myself critically and wrinkled my nose in a sneer. Not looking my best.

I could barely make out one of the tube lines' little control boxes outside on the wall of the tunnel, its dim red light flashing above my reflection's right ear. The woman to my left turned the page of her newspaper with a dry hissing sound. The woman four seats to my right crossed her legs. She was wearing leopard print leggings. They were distorted in the window, like her heavily shaded eyelids and bright red lips. I surreptitiously glanced at her down the carriage, her large brown hand held tight by the small white fingers of the man next to her. Tattoos snaked up both of their arms, and his face was as colourfully made up as hers, all violent streaks of colour and dark lines. I think I was probably envious of their carelessness. They didn't care that it was dangerous to stand out these days. For them I guess it was worth the risk. Whereas I couldn't stop the fear, compulsively checking my reflection in shop windows and mirrors, checking: am I too obvious?

Am I nondescript? Do I fade into the background, do people's eyes slide over me as though I'm not even there? The constant safety checks chasing themselves around inside my brain like the subway trains on their closed loops.

I wondered what we looked like from outside by the control box, a grey, graffiti-ridden coffin filled with grey, graffiti-ridden zombies. And me, just a beige zombie in a pink cardigan and old grey leggings that had worn out their elasticity. The woman beside me was wearing something so similar I wouldn't be surprised if she'd bought it in the same thrift store. I wondered if everyone else was as scared as I was. If the fear that I felt lay heavily over the city these days permeated their lives as desperately as it did mine. Were they checking mirrors too?

Finally, the train shuddered and groaned into motion again, its wheels squealing as the brakes released. I was staring at my reflection again, thinking it was strange how the curved glass made it look like I was two feet tall, when I finally realised what my eyes had been telling my brain, what it had refused to hear.

My breath went slow, shallow, as I finally looked straight at the reflection of the woman beside me. Her eyes were the same ones I'd seen every day, in all those countless, fruitless mirror checks. The line of her jaw and the creases across her forehead, the small red mole under her left eye, were all terrifyingly familiar. I stared with sick fascination, and that's how I broke the first rule: *don't let them see you've seen.* She looked up at me, straight into my eyes, and winked.

My heart thudded in my chest like it was trying to get out and my whole body slammed back into my seat. I let my face go slack, blank, and stared hard past the reflection and out at the shiny ductwork reflecting the train's lights as we streamed past, trying to shield the way my mind was racing.

I caught sight of the leopard print lady looking at my reflection in the carriage. Her brown eyes slid sideways to the reflection beside me and horrified realisation dawned on her face. She gasped and her eyes flicked straight ahead, staring dumbly out of the window and squeezing her boyfriend's hand tightly enough that her knuckles popped loudly in the silence. The train made a howling noise as it changed track.

The woman's eyes slid inexorably back to mine, like she couldn't help herself, and softened with fear and helpless sympathy as she saw the hopeless desperation in mine. She shook her head slowly and mouthed 'I'm sorry,' before determinedly looking away again.

My heart pounded so hard I could feel my breath stutter in my lungs. I was alone. I didn't – couldn't – take it personally. We all knew the rules. *Don't stand out, don't give them a reason to notice you. Kill the second twin. Don't let your children play dress up. Don't let them see you've seen. Don't make contact. Run, and be thankful it isn't you.* But that didn't stop the forlorn hope picking at the heart of my despair. *Save me*, I pleaded. *Someone, anyone.* Why had it chosen me? What had I done?

I'd always been so careful, so diffident, so heartlessly timid and dull. Why hadn't it picked someone braver and more foolish like the colourful couple down the carriage? Why not them?

I hated myself for thinking so cruelly, so selfishly. But when we're afraid, we grasp at anything to convince ourselves this can't be right. Someone, somewhere made a mistake. But there was no mistake. The reflection was mine, and it knew I knew. Now I only had to wait. It didn't matter where. I could stay on this tube until the end of the line and ride it all the way back again, or get off a stop early and walk home through the roughest bit of the estate alone, or go home and sit on the sofa and wait. It didn't matter. It was coming for me.

That is, if the Catchers didn't get me first. The leopard print woman was staring blankly at her phone – who knew if she'd raised the alarm already? Signal down there was spotty, but there were always ways to attract their attention.

I sat rigidly in my seat, determinedly staring straight at my own eyes and out of the window as the train moaned through the passages, steadfastly ignoring the taunting gaze of my other reflection.

There were no Catchers waiting on the platform at the next station, ready to swarm in and neutralise in their white, helmeted uniforms. Just an old man with a beagle. As soon as the doors opened, the leopard print woman and her boyfriend jumped up and hurriedly exited the train. Her head twitched as they stepped onto the platform, like she wanted to look back but caught herself at the last minute. The man with the dog got onto the next carriage.

We rattled on past another three empty stations, my two reflections and I, both of them staring at me while I held the gaze of only one. Finally we reached my stop and I got up, staggering slightly before the weakness in my knees subsided, and walked past the empty seat beside me and out of the train.

And now what? My heels click on the tiled floor as I walk away from the platform, filling the bright white pedestrian tunnels with the sharp sound, like scissors snipping. My reflection follows me in the plastic pane-covered billboards, bobbing through advertisements and missing persons posters. In the dull reflection off the white tiles I see a second shadow keep pace with me.

As I reach the terminus and the row of turnstiles gingerly edges out from behind the corner I hear the sound of a second pair of heels. *Click-click, click-click.* I don't turn to look. I swipe my transit card to exit the station, and climb the steps to street level.

The footsteps follow me. The cool breeze hits my skin and raises goosebumps on my arms. Where shall I go? I look down the road at the park, and the row of greasy cafes that lead down toward where there is music, where restaurants and nightclubs huddle together against the cold and dance with light. Is that where I want to go? Do? What do I like to do? It hits me that I've spent so long trying not to be visible to Them that I've forgotten what I look like inside. I don't know what I like to do. I don't know what I enjoy. Music? Food? Company? I don't even have friends.

The footsteps wait patiently.

I turn away from the park, and people, and walk toward home. I guess I haven't really lived before, so I don't know. Will I miss it?

I walk more confidently tonight, no longer afraid of what might be in the overwhelming face of what is. At least for just one night, I'm only afraid of one singular shadow.

The footsteps sound closer now, more defined. Like they have form. I breathe deeply and sigh into the night air, my heart beating in my throat. There is nothing left to fear. It is coming for me.

GENRE-FLUID

31

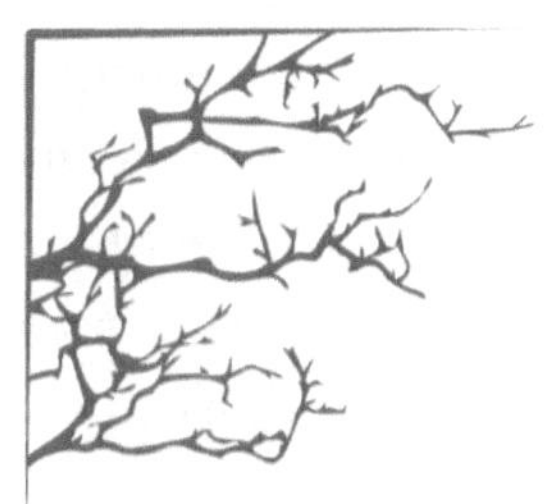

Eet

THE MOMENT OF IMPACT; the shuddering roll of a body; the smashing of bones and blood vessels and life. The eyes through the windscreen, wide in pain, in shock, suddenly lost, dulled, gone, empty. The sound of the screams coming from your own mouth.

You wake up, starting awake and staring wide at the ceiling. Your bedsheets are soaked with sweat, hot and cold and wet on your skin. Your hands start steady, then shake as they come up to wipe your face. You sit up, out of the swimming sheets, and swing your feet onto the floor. The cool night air chills you, the sweat rapidly cooling on your skin. You want to stand, remove yourself from your disgusting bed, but you stay glued in place. The messages go to your legs to pull you up, put you on your pale feet, but they do not respond.

Finally, you break out of your reverie and force yourself to stand. The shower calls to you and you stumble through the dark room towards the bathroom light switch, stubbing your toe on the doorframe. Hissing through your teeth, you lean on the wall to regain your balance before turning on the light.

Immediately, the sterile bathroom is flooded with brittle white, leaving spots in front of your sleep-darkened eyes. When you blink, they look like headlights. You turn the dial for the shower and it pours out cold water. It warms quickly and you step in, pulling the curtain across and belatedly remembering your towel on the floor in the bedroom. The water slowly changes from warm to hot to scalding. You stay under, relishing the sting on your skin, the mind-numbing spatters of pain combatting the throbbing ache in your toe. You don't know which hurts more.

Clean, you step out of the shower and brace against the cold air, groping for your towel in the dim backlight from the bathroom door. You quickly rub it over your face, arms and chest, towelling your hair roughly before wrapping it around your waist. Water drips cold down your back and it feels like the sweat you were covered in earlier. You shudder, wriggling your shoulders, and shake some of the water off. The display on your alarm clock, sideways and on the floor, reads 3:15. You don't think you can sleep again, so you turn on your bedroom light at last, and consider changing the bedding. The thought of lying back down in it repulses you. It is two hours before dawn. What else do you have to do at this time but marinate in your thoughts?

You change your bedding and marinate anyway. The inquiry is looming – you've never been to court before, never even had jury duty – and you vaguely worry about what to wear. What does it matter? You could wear a dishcloth or a pinstripe suit, it wouldn't change how guilty you are. Your lawyer assured you that you'll get off, it was just a desperate accident, the jury will agree. They'll vindicate you. You didn't even try to care. A jury of your peers, a judge, a lawyer. The whole bloody world could forgive you, God himself could stamp on your record 'Not Guilty' and it wouldn't change a jot. It would not remove a single atom of this crushing, deathlike demon on your chest.

A part of you feels like everything so far has been a dream, or someone's terrible idea of a practical joke, but the rest has accepted it surprisingly calmly. It has happened, and you must deal with it. You are methodical in your daily life, going through the motions of living, but you're still waiting to wake up. The day everything happened in pairs. A little piece of you that you're ashamed of whispers *'it would have been easier if it had only been one or the other'* and then suggests that the crash would have been the easier option. You cringe away from it and try to ignore it, but the thought is there, irrepressible and wrong. A life is worth more than a love. You think.

You're not entirely sure if Rachael knows what happened. You haven't spoken since you drove off after she told you it was the end. You certainly don't want her to know. Or maybe you do; she would be kind and understanding and maybe you could try again. You hate yourself for thinking of a child's death as an opportunity to try to rekindle your dead relationship. No one has told you the name of the boy, but you remember so distinctly his mother screaming it as he ran out straight in front of you. *Jack. Jack. Jack.* His father's instant reaction to run out after his son, to scoop him back up into his arms and out of harm's way, unable to catch a fast, determined child on the run. One second was all it would have taken; one second's difference. If the heartbreaking stillness after the breakup had lasted just a moment longer, you could have seen it happening, could have slammed on the brakes faster, stopped in time, and Jack would have gotten a scolding for running out, and sausages and beans for dinner. Even if you had been a second earlier, Jack would have run into the side of your car and bounced off, maybe a broken foot under a tyre, or he would have stopped as you went past in front of his nose, run back to mummy and daddy frightened, bruised and crying, but alive.

If Rachael hadn't chosen that day to tell you what she did, then the scene would never have appeared at all. You bite back that response; *Rachael* did nothing wrong. It hurts to know that you aren't absolutely in the right and she is not absolutely in the wrong, but you know she had the right to end it. It means facing the fact that she just *doesn't want you*; there is nothing you can 'fix' or 'make better' or use to persuade her: she just can't be with you any more. That doesn't stop you asking where you went wrong, when you started pushing away, what you could have done differently to keep her, but you know it is the truth, however much you want it to be a lie.

You slump back on your clean bedding and stare back up at the ceiling's cracks. You roll onto your side, then back again, then sit up straight and throw yourself back down again. The erratic movements don't help but they summarise, they perform how wildly hurt and bewildered you are. The guilt feels like a piledriver, rising above everything else and swamping you like your sweaty old bedclothes. Everything else, even Rachael leaving you, pales in comparison. You want so much to be able to press backspace, eet, rewind, reverse, anything to change what happened. You wish you had headed to the bar before driving away, that you had gotten drunk and killed yourself on a lamppost on the way home, the bonnet crumpling and curling around it, leaving no one hurt but you and the council budget. You wish you had stopped outside the off license on the way home to get drunk there, delayed your journey by even a minute. You wish you had decided to go Zen and drive to the viewpoint and waited for the stars to come out to comfort you with their uncaring, breathlessly cold beauty. But you didn't. And you cannot change that. You cannot take back Jack's mother's tears, his father's broken sobs. You cannot breathe life back into that little, crumpled body. You cannot save him. You cannot save anyone.

Your alarm starts violently beeping and you jump; has it been three hours already? You roll over and reach down to turn it off before it starts to sound like a heart monitor. You roll back and only then do you notice the light creeping in through the curtains. An hour past dawn. Another day. A day closer to the court, another day without Rachael. Another day without Jack.

GABRIEL OAKTHORN

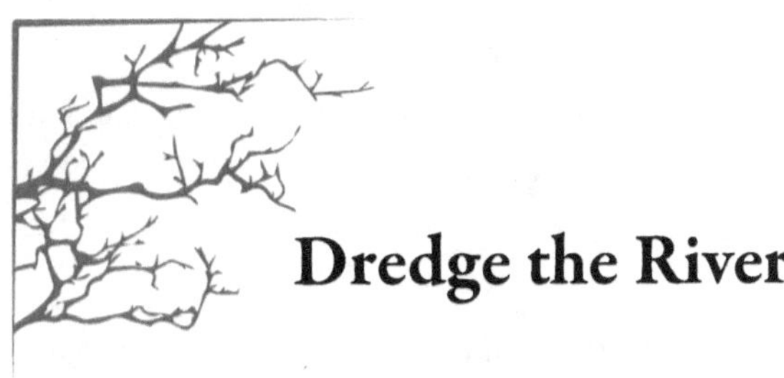

Dredge the River

I WOKE UP A NEW MAN today. For the 3587th time. Not that I'm counting.

I groan into the morning, wishing I could ruffle my hair into casual celebrity cuteness, maybe stretch aesthetically, yawn with sweet breath and doze as the sun paints stripes across me. Instead, I roll clumsily out of bed and awkwardly waddle to the bathroom. My dad tells me on days like today I should stand to pee, have some pride in my masculinity, but I sit down anyway. Not like it'd stop him laughing at me. It's neater this way, and I'm used to it.

I yawn, and shudder at the taste of my own mouth – that, at least, never changes. The toothpaste hits my tongue like a balm. Tingly-fresh breath, delivered in an unrecyclable plastic tube. I catch sight of myself between the white spots on the mirror and pull a face, mouth distorted by my chewed-up toothbrush.

The changes are subtle. Cheekbones a little sharper than yesterday, jawline more defined. A hint of stubble across my chin. Even my chest is flatter, collarbone sculpted. Maybe it's all in my head. At least my eyes don't change, or my hair. Always blue, always black. Less changes than stays the same. The bump in my nose, too big some days, just right on others; hands, androgynously long and slender regardless; feet too big to find shoes.

I spit into the sink.

My wardrobe intimidates me. I had this cute dress all picked out for today and now I'm not sure I'm feeling it. Not many guys get away with summer dresses where I'm going. Shorts it is.

I fiddle with my hair in the cloudy mirror, putting off going downstairs until my parents leave. I haven't had a day like this in three and a half weeks, and Dad won't be happy about me breaking my new record. He loves both of me, but he can't stand the transitions. It forces him to remember his kid's not what he expected them to be.

Mum nicknamed me 'Orlando'. She says it's like having a Woolf character for a kid. I guess I should be grateful my real name can be shortened to a genderless 'Art'. I think she hoped my life would be full of it.

I immediately regret not wearing the dress. The sun borders on vengeful and I'm already sweating like cheese at a picnic. The bus drives past me. I'm standing like a girl, could be gay. Slumping against the stop sign, I screw my eyes shut against the brightness and feel my nose sizzle. I forgot sunscreen.

An hour and four sweaty buses later, I'm belched out by the last – and clunkiest – into the industrial estate. Funny how buses get older and wheezier the further into the old town you get. Like they're trying for authenticity.

A stumbling posse of footie fans with flags on their faces starts chanting something rhythmic and loud. I stick my head down and walk away slowly enough to not look afraid.

The old bridge is abandoned, as usual. Something about the 'Warning: Dodgy Everything' signs keeps people away. I duck through the gap in the fence and follow the railway tracks onto the maintenance platform in the middle of the bridge.

The river flows sluggishly and stinks in the heat. Downtown is upstream, so here's where all that filth people think the river will magic away gets clogged. Plastic bottles, diapers, takeaway boxes... the dragging tree branches are rich with refuse.

I sit and gently boil in the sun. Midsummer isn't the best time to come here, but it's tradition. Five years go by fast when you're not looking. This is where I catch them. Cast my nets into the river and dredge up the jumbled memories that snag on the branches like litter.

Five years ago I came here with a very specific intention. I didn't think I'd ever come back, let alone five more times. It was overcast – one of those heavy, damp summers where everyone wishes it was hot enough to start complaining. No sunshine on the water, just a brittle kind of clarity that highlighted all the muck lurking down there. It would've been a quick thing, probably, but disgusting.

I stand up and step forwards, toes to the edge. The rusted fence has been eaten by salt. I look down into the water, like I did back then, and I don't feel dizzy this time either. I guess when you've spent hours imagining jumping off something you stop being scared of falling off it.

It was the muck that changed my mind. I didn't want to be just another piece of trash dredged out of the estuary. Funny, the things that call you back.

I step back and sit down. Just because I'm not afraid anymore doesn't mean I want to risk joining the refuse pile anyway. I'm past that.

It's funny. People want to know what's on my birth certificate, what's between my legs, but it wouldn't help them understand. It's not like anything's permanent anyway. I've spent my whole life dealing with other people's reactions to what happens to me, like their thoughts matter in the grand scheme of what I'm dealing with every day. Like my body is something happening to them, rather than just being the place where I live.

The sun really is hot. My t-shirt sticks to my back and my scalp itches. A part of me wants to stay longer, for remembrance, but the rest of me dreams of ice cream. Maybe I should think about where I'm going rather than where I've been - if ice cream is in my future, it can't be all bad.

I stand up and wipe my hands on my shorts, grimacing at the dampness. As I stride back the way I came, my body loosens, easing back into its shape. One thing's for sure, no matter how I wake up. Tomorrow I'm going to wear the dress.

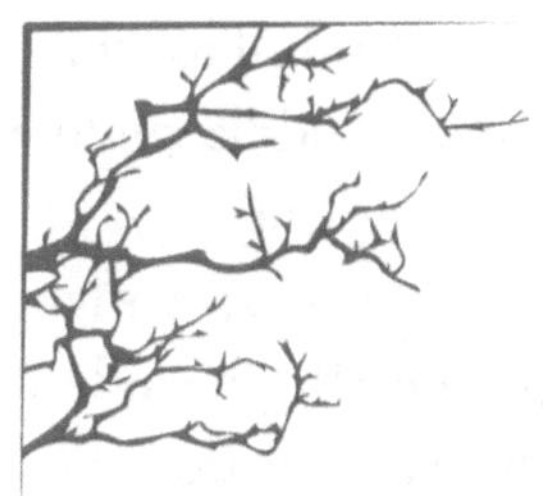

7 a.m.

SEVEN A.M. AND THE righteous of the world are only just waking up. The dawn light is dusty, gold-speckled. What am I doing here? The city lies before me, lit by the rising sun, as I, breathless, clamber up the side of this never-ending hill.

My lungs ache, air coming in short bursts as my straining legs push me up ever further. One foot in front of the other foot. I wouldn't be here if I hadn't made a stupid bet. A part of me wants to curse the man I said those fateful words to, but that would feel uncharitable. He can't help being a doubter. I didn't even know his name. Thomas, perhaps.

There is some small glory, I admit, in being the last one up. The others all went home hours ago, drained and laughing at me in my stubbornness. But I will see this through. An awareness settles on my shoulders like a cape – I am doing this for all of us, those who fell before, as well as myself.

Ugh, self-righteous, vain twat. It was only a night out, for Christ's sake. No one's bloody died. God, my legs ache.

I want to rest, catch my breath. Maybe check out the already glorious sunrise behind me. But if I stop now, I'll never reach the top. Love Hill for sunrise was a stupid wager. Why couldn't I have gone for the rooftop terrace? At least that way I'd still be able to get a drink.

I could still turn round. Head back down the hill to where the others are, no doubt curled up in some cuddle puddle without me. I wonder if they even notice I'm missing.

Residual tracers haunt my vision, remnants of a night where the stars sang and melted down the sky in endless fractals. Only they do have an end. I'm just chasing after their tails now.

There aren't any stars left. It's just the one. The big, overripe, red sun, casting his too-serious, judgemental glow down on us.

Why is the sun male? When did we decide that the sun, bright and eternal, was a man, while his subservient, transient reflection was the epitome of femininity? I'd rather be a moon than the sun. At least then I'd get some sleep.

I don't know why I'm complaining. I'm happy, really, here by myself, labouring up this hill to see a sunrise at the dusk of my own personal day. I must be very lucky to be here, witnessing this splendour. My gentle, fried brain whispers shyly to me of my own magnificent role in this tableau, and I feel godlike. A shiver runs through me and I realise I'm well over thirteen hours past what my friend Jordy would call 'T'. The comedown. T plus thirteen hours. No wonder I'm starting to feel the cold again. I'm only wearing a thin t-shirt and jeans, my jumper discarded hours before around the shoulders of some beautiful young creature I couldn't bear to see so covered in naked goosebumps. I have no idea where he went, but he took my last warm layer with him.

Bastard, I think warmly. What a beautiful, selfish being. I love him.

My mind glances back over the people I spent the majority of the night with, and loves them too. Marie, Jordy's recent girlfriend with her self-conscious stretchmarks and wide eyes, so eager to be crazy and young despite the two babies her slender frame has borne. Red-eyed stoner Mark, with whom I share an occasional joint and sometimes something more. Fucking hippie. He's a white boy with greasy dreadlocks and I can't stand to touch them except when I'm high.

I glance at my hands and they still crawl with paisley and fleur de lis, starbursts of colour spiralling between the pores, vibrancy swirling under my flesh. There's a layer of grime engrained in my fingerprints, throwing them into sharp relief. What complex patterns they are. I nearly stop there, staring at my hands.

But a cool breeze shudders through me and I force myself to keep walking, keep thinking. Who have I thought of? What have I missed out? The beautiful thief; Marie of the mussed red lipstick; Jordy of the ridiculous backward baseball caps; Mark of the cigarette-shaped pipes. He bought them in Amsterdam.

I shake my head. Who have I missed? I must think of them all or they won't be here to watch the sunrise with me. They'll be in a bed somewhere, at home perhaps, and won't see how beautiful this morning will be when it finally breaks. Not that they'll be with me anyway, but it's the thought that counts. It's the... synchronicity. I want to believe we share that, at least. It would be nice to be synchronous with someone.

Thelma. She always feels incomplete without her Louise. I introduced her to every Louise I knew, just for a laugh, but none of them stuck. She obviously needs a different kind of Velcro. Thelma, who'd disappeared two hours in, caused us all to panic, and showed up after another hour, having apparently been staring at herself in the bathroom mirror. I find mirrors are best avoided on nights like these. I become enraptured with myself, enchanted by my own eyes. I look deeply into my perfect, black pupils and forgive every wrong I have ever done to me. It can take hours, or seconds. I only really notice when someone drags me out of it.

Mirrors are for the days when you can't stand to look at yourself.

God, does this hill never end? I don't remember it taking so long last time. But the gentle pink streaks of the sky catch my eye and wink, as though they know something I don't. A stunning droplet of dew lingering on a blade of grass glistens invitingly, and I stop to take a closer look. I will get there when I get there.

After only five minutes of silent, adoring contemplation, my legs start me walking again. It takes me by surprise, a little bit. I wasn't expecting to keep going. But this adventure is important. It must be had, this experience. Or else it won't be had, by anyone. If not me, then who? If not now, then when? My brain takes me for a gentle stroll around my own whirlpooling thoughts. I think in spirals, in Fibonacci strands and the centres of sunflowers. I would like to be a sunflower, and always turn my face to the sun. Maybe the sun is male because I like it, and I like men.

It's possible.

Shit, this was strong stuff. The pink streaks in the sky are brighter now, deeper colours, and they're setting off my acid washed blue brain like fireworks. I could do with some music.

My hands fumble in my pockets for headphones, taking an age to locate them. Millennia pass as I pull them out and attempt to untangle them. I swear an eon creeps by behind my back as I stick the jack into my phone.

My legs are slowing, pausing as I scroll through my stored music, determined to locate just the right piece to sum up everything I'm feeling. It's a frustrating endeavour.

Eventually my thumbs, knowing better than my brain, pick out 'Heavyweight'. I wonder briefly if I'm being grandiose. As the first bell of the track tolls, I close my eyes, savouring the taste of the song's fluency. It feels like blackberries in my mouth, ripe and juicy and bursting with Technicolor sound.

I open my eyes and force my legs to start moving again. My body feels disjointed, slow and syrupy. It longs for sleep, but my eyes and my brain are still too taken up with jittery, joy-filled, anxious, twitching thoughts. Comedowns are endless sometimes.

I glance into the future and see the next two days of recovery, just lying on my bed wrapped in a duvet with empty pizza boxes strewn around, too lazy to cook and too absorbed in some Netflix show to care. Jordy will probably invite me out again tomorrow night but like hell am I doing this twice in a row. Twice in a month is more than enough.

The brow of the hill looks like it's coming closer towards me faster than I am moving towards it. Strange sensation, this walking thing. My footsteps tramp to the beat of the song, and I make little 'wah wah' noises with my too-damp, too-dry mouth along with the vocals.

My tongue feels weird. I think I'm thirsty. Why didn't I bring water with me? Thelma was so good all night, making sure everyone stayed hydrated, bringing us offerings of water in cups and bottles, little tributes on her altar to her friends. I love Thelma. She might be my favourite human being. It's not impossible.

I love them all, though. People are beautiful and terrible, cruel and cruelty-free. A snippet of conversation strikes a discordant note through my thoughts and I try not to dwell on it, but when the beautiful creature who stole my jumper looked deep into my eyes and said 'you're tripping balls, aren't you?' I can't tell if it was disgusted or admiring or neutral and it bothers me still.

It doesn't matter, he doesn't matter. Fuck him. Don't fuck him. I chase myself around into a slow spiral of admiration for his perfect form and gentle eyes. A being so pure couldn't have felt anything as base as disgust for another creature. I hope the world treats him well. I hope he enjoys my jumper. I wish I had my jumper. The chill's really starting to set into my fingertips and I can't stop shaking, though I don't feel cold.

But was he disgusted though? No, surely- but maybe- no, he was cute- what does that have anything to do with it- I'm not- he's not, I'm not, not, not, it's ok but I'm tired and wow this sunrise is bright and just- stop whirlpooling and enjoy this moment.

I keep walking, full of wonder and delight at the dawn, and then fall back into the spiral.

Ugh. I love this but after thirteen hours it's tiring. When can I sleep? When the drugs let me- wear off- dry out? Dry out? Where did that come from? Maybe I can only sleep when I'm asleep and my brain's caught unawares. That's ridiculous.

The scuff of my shoe against my calf distracts me, grounds me. It hurts, kind of, but not badly. Everything feels good to some degree. That's why we manifest it. Is that true or is that bullshit? I don't know anymore. Maybe I never knew.

I take a deep breath and the colours wash over me again, thoughts dizzying me like the perfect geometrics I see, gently spinning.

You know- there's only so much- I don't think I'm gonna- of my thoughts I can really- do acid again for a- whiiil- thinnn- whi- thi- while- think- think?

My thoughts feel like my breathing; harsh and- harsh and stuttering and fast and slow and very, very gentle. I'm a living oxymoron. A contradiction in terms. It's not like there are rules for this stuff. Breathing, thinking. All that matters is you keep doing it.

A dog and its walker approach me. The world zeroes in and forces me to admit that their presence alarms me. I give them a reassuring- manic- smile and pretend I think they think I'm sober.

To my relief, the dog ignores me and lumbers on past. I don't think I could deal with a conversation right now. The owner, I'm sure, is giving me a sidelong-concerned-judgemental glance on her way past.

I want to tell her how wonderful everything is but she'd just think I'm high. I *am* high. Funny how hard it is to remember that.

Even after this long, it's always like the first time, denying you're feeling it until you really can't pretend your swirling vision is normal anymore, praying for it to last forever and end right *now*. I guess we're all just reluctant to leave a present state. Sober or flying, it doesn't matter. We just want to maintain our personal status quo.

Maybe we're all just as afraid of change as the labels on baristas' tip jars say.

Fear. Recently I feel that I only get high to mitigate- counteract- hide from (like a coward) the fear I feel about this unfriendly world we are building for ourselves.

We voted out of a common dream of utopia, a madman elected to the helm, the powers of the world flex their muscles in an ostentatious show of strength.

Are we on the brink?

Maybe every generation feels like this.

I feel my brain start to slip down the rabbit hole and red pill blue pill- blue pill *stop*.

It's okay. I have done something to my brain. I have made it high. Soon it will be low. Or at least normal. What is normal? This is not normal, this seeing fleur de lis painted across the sky. That's good. Focus on how beautiful everything is. That's better than war- famine- disease- stop it. Pretty things. *Focus*.

How tall is this hill? When did I stop walking?

I make myself move forwards as the next song on my playlist starts. It's a good transition. I remember listening to this song, curled up around my friend Bee, the first time I tried a research chem in the wrong setting, and how when he played this song in our shared pair of headphones all I could hear in that one ear was glory. That night was the first time the lines between my body and another's blurred away. I could feel fingertips on my arm where I idly caressed his skin, lips on my neck as I earnestly kissed his. It was almost religious.

These are good memories. It's funny how each trip feels like dipping back into the world of a previous one. Not all are in the same reality, but there are always places we go to each time that feel like home. Sometimes I miss home.

Maybe that's another reason to trip. Everywhere becomes home when you belong to everything.

My aunt talks of champagne and the men who bought it for her. I wonder why there is no one to buy *me* champagne. Sometimes I wish that I, too, had been nestled in that prosecco bubble world of iridescent gowns and starched suits, a child given hatboxes and shuttlecocks to play with, corks and diamonds to teethe on.

Instead I'm here, a washed up ghost of a night under harsh lights and soft nimbuses. A slithering, pale creature left out to dry in the morning sun.

I close my eyes and rest the backs of my hands on my knees. My acid brain repeats the truth to me of my own transcendence. I shrug the thoughts out as best I can, their persistent repetition and exultant chiming irritating now. Acid and ego, ago and acid. It's- you're- unbearable if you're not careful. T plus thirteen and a half hours. At least the brow of the hill is within reach now. I can see the bench on its crest from here. The last push. The final frontier.

How many ears did Spock have? Left, right and final front-ear. Who told me that? Jordy's ex-girlfriend loved shitty jokes. It was probably her.

She had a Polish friend who was a roadie for this band once, but she always wanted a Czech one too, Czech one two. Labracadabrador. That's not relevant. Maybe the dog earlier was a labracadabrador and that was why it ignored me. Too busy doing magic things.

'I'm here.' The voice almost makes me jump, even though it's my own. How did my brain slip that one past me?

I stop where I stand, eyes closed, right by the bench at the prow of the hill. I came here once with a girlfriend, back before I realised I was more interested in her brother. It would be weirdly perfect if she showed up now. Like fate.

Actually it would just be bloody awkward.

I take a deep breath of the cool, crisp air and say goodbye to the rainbow Volkswagen symbols swimming behind my eyelids. Opening my eyes, I almost want to cry with splendour.

It's like something out of a fairytale. A broken, urban fantasy with fairies with 'Fe' and iron molecules tattooed on their skin.

The red sun has risen fully now above the horizon, setting the city's windows sparkling. Rose-tinted vapour trails streak across the sky like the tracers of a lover's fingertips. Further out, the fields are hazy under a light dew-breath. A gentle, misty moisty morning. I can see the sea's glimmer in the distance.

Picture-perfect. Crystal. Frozen. I breathe deeply and cough. Mark and his bloody joints. He knows my lungs don't take it, but he always offers. And when I'm seeing paisley across his skin and paradise in his blown pupils I never say no. I'm a slut on psychedelics. Thelma teases me for it but I don't mind. It's nice, falling in love easily with everyone I meet, and the heartbreaks last less than a minute – when rainbows coat the world, when beauty- when truth- God-everything is so clear, how can one be sad?

When everything looks like... this.

A spiderweb catches my eye, stretched taut and wearing diamonds. I step closer, careful not to walk too fast in case I ruin it. My breath mists softly, cloudlike, around it, and the fat, sleek spider vibrates in her web. She's beautiful. I want to reach out and touch her, so I do. She doesn't like it much and skitters away, towards the scant shelter supplied by the scrubby leaves fringing her private city.

'Sorry,' I murmur. That was a faux pas. Don't touch spiders- people- anyone-without asking. 'Have a good morning.' I straighten and look back at the sunrise, squinting tightly against the brightness. It hurts my overblown pupils, still dilated despite the time. T plus fourteen hours, I suppose. No wonder I'm so tired.

As if on cue, my body sinks with weariness and I stagger to the bench, collapsing slowly, creakingly onto it. It's cold and damp through my jeans, prickling my skin. I want to be at home, wrapped up in my duvet. I want to sink into warmth and sleep. Maybe creep into Jordy's room and snuggle down with him and Marie, feel warm, bed-heavy limbs tangled with my own for a few hours.

But first, I have to walk there.

Hallelujah

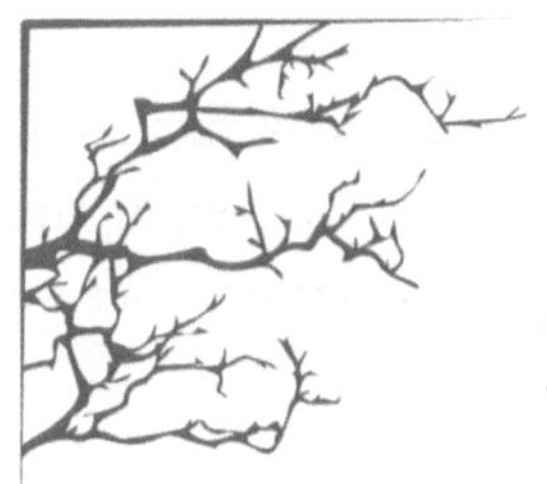

THE FUNERAL WAS A SIMPLE affair. The procession wound down through the dusty summer streets, the entire village following the wicker coffin except the Silents scattering dead flowers on the road before it, harbingers dressed all in white. Marje followed, holding her mother's hand, watching the wheels of the coffincart rumble and crack and stick in the ruts.

The priest spoke his words of comfort, the honest, plain words of a country man who believed in nothing more than love and gentleness. He performed the rite to return Marje's father's energy to the earth at sunset. Once the first star was spotted, the pyre was lit, and the flames flickered into the night, sending sparks flying up hundreds of feet into the air. Marje could see the dancing fire reflected in the eyes of her mother, shining in the tears on her cheeks. She turned back to the pyre, and stood watching until the embers were nothing but a faint glow.

The tribe left for home, sad and murmuring condolences to her mother. They stayed, Marje and her mother. They sat together on the cold, damp ground, beside the glowing embers. They didn't speak for a long time. Then Marje poked one of the brightest, closest embers with a stick, and a little flame leapt back up, looking glad to be woken up again.

'Look, Mama, Da's saying hello.'

'So he is.' Her mother's voice sounded choked, like she'd inhaled a sweet instead of swallowing it. Marje waved at the little flame, which danced for a moment longer before disappearing.

'Will he come and visit us sometimes?' The little girl didn't look at her mother; she didn't like seeing her cry. It made her want to hit things. But there was nothing to hit; she was crying because Da had died and was going to live in the air and the ground and the trees again.

'He's in everything now, love.' Her mother hugged her tight, pulling her close under the cloak they shared. 'He's in the rainbows. Whenever you see a rainbow, that's your Da telling you to smile.'

Marje thought about this for a moment. 'What if he comes when I'm asleep?'

'You'll know, Marje.'

Marje thought about the white flower she'd put in the coffin with her father. It was the nicest one she could find. One of the Silents had smiled at her when she put it in. They didn't smile often. She felt her mother's arms tighten around her and looked into the fire, leaning back against her. The slowly rippling amber of the embers made her sleepy, and eventually her head tipped forward and she slept.

They stayed sat by the fire until dawn, as tradition demanded, and a bit longer to watch the sun rise fully over the hills. Marje's mother woke her up to see. It was beautiful and bright, and the birds sang as happily as they usually did. Marje wondered if her Da was singing with them. She asked her mother.

'Yes, dearheart. He's out there somewhere, singing as loudly as he can so you know he's there.' She didn't say anything else, so Marje stood up to have a look at the ashes. They were still warm, and there were a few embers left hot, so she didn't touch them after the first one. The thought that she was walking through the remains of her father's body didn't bother her; he was still warm and welcoming, and close. The ash swirled around her feet and warmed her boots. The sky was a pale, clear blue above, and the grass outside of the burnt circle was green and yellow with summer.

She looked to the east, and the sun left spots in her vision, a bright yellow orb climbing above the horizon. To the north she saw the mountains, tinged with fire, like the pyre, in the morning sun. The west was a riot of hills and fields, stubble and ash now, after the harvest and the burning. The south faded away into the distance, where a blue blur showed the sea. And there she was, in the middle of all of it; in the middle of the world, under the big blue bowl of the sky.

There Da had lived, and there he had been returned to the world. It glowed in the sun, and she decided it was Da waving again. She stood in the middle of the pyre and stretched out her arms, reaching from one end of the horizon to the other.

'Marje, what are you doing?' her mother called.

'I'm hugging Da!' she called back. 'He's in everything!'

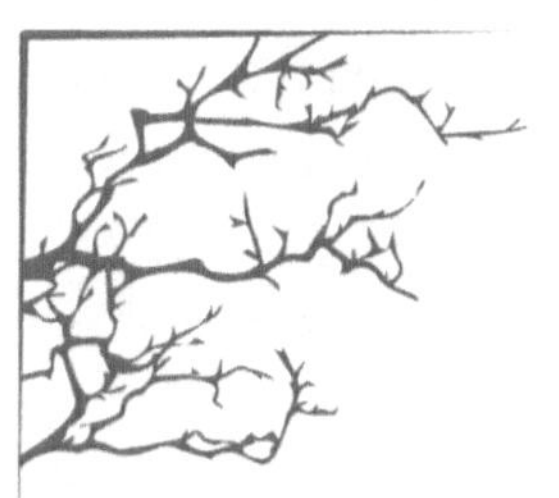

Warder

THE BANGING HASN'T stopped all night. It's hard to tell if it's coming from inside your head or the door that's shaking in its frame with every thud. The light fittings shudder, shaken clear of a decade's worth of dust and congealed cigarette smoke. The grey dullness of morning filters through the blinds, paints your boy in stripes like the severe bars of a jail. He shouldn't be here, not with you. You screw your eyes tight shut against the colours snaking across his skin, but they fly open again at the shock of the next harsh beat of the fist on the other side of the door.

You check your watch. Ten minutes since he started. You sniff and rub your eyes fiercely, grinding the smokeburn deeper into the redness. Maybe no one is out to get you. Ten minutes is too long for the cops but not for a drunk. Your time perception is askew. Ten minutes since the banging started, and ten hours. Fifteen minutes since your last line. Three hours since your last spliff. Forty two since you were sober enough to leave the flat.

Dark, furious energy emanates from the peeling red paint. Angry faces in the Artex swirls on the ceiling, creeping insects in the dust between the writhing floorboards. Rats possessed by devils in the piles of stale junk food wrappers. It's not real, can't be real, but it still feels believable. You can't fight the fear.

You wonder if the banging is real, if anything is real except what's in your system, keeping you awake and dirtying your mind and making it so clear to you that you are a sinner. When did the door last look like you remember it? How long has it been since you dived too deep?

The banging stops long enough for you to hear the grumbling like your cavernous stomach. The silence is eerie and unnerving, the breath before the scream. Are those footsteps? Is he leaving? How long has he been standing there, banging to be let in? Eleven minutes. How long since you last ate anything more than crisps and mouldy salsa and the bitter backdrip after a new line? Swallowed anything more than paper squares and fungus?

Your boy's curled up on the mildewing brown sofa, wrapped in Slab's filthy coat. That, at least, was something he left behind. Your littlee looks so small under the expanse of dirty, grey fabric, like an exposed heart in tissue paper. Soft, brown hair falls into his eyes and obscures the finger pressed against the side of his nose. You know he's sucking his thumb, know he never listens to your threats of buck teeth and lisps. He needs comfort, and after you threw his Bugsy out of the window in a fit of demonic possession, his thumb's the best he can get.

Water drips from an icicle hanging sullenly off a broken pipe. Landlord hasn't been to fix the heating yet. You're surprised there isn't a matching one dangling below your nose. You rub it with a hand. Nothing. Just more white dust. Your breath clouds in the air like the sea fog that rolled in yesterday and blanketed you into staying in this town despite your highway of good intentions. The banging resumes.

You need a joint. Aching, stiff fingers fumble in the pockets of your coat, shaking from the high and the comedown. Your eyelids droop despite the noise, and your hand stills. How long have you been awake? Your body's a neglected mess. A pile of old cracks and sinew, stringing your deep-cold skeleton together like so much wispy cloud. Is this dying?

The thought sends demonic fractal influence spiralling behind your eyelids and you fling them open like damp-swollen windows. You sniff and it drips down the back of your throat, bitter and unyielding like the devils that haven't stopped swirling in your vision just because you opened the lids they hide behind.

'Five,' you say, like your boy taught you. Five things you can see. 'KFC wrappers; peacock eyes everywhere; angel feathers; light through stripy blinds.' You sigh and look at him, and you love how the air around him ripples and radiates. 'And my boy.'

Your fingers awaken again and root around in your pockets for the last of your tobacco. Damp papers stick to them and you shake one loose onto the coffee-granule and crumbs floor that you gave up on promising to vacuum months ago. You scrounge up some moist, linty tobacco from the depths of your pocket, all jumbled in with the last of your bud. The sheen over your eyes even makes that mess look beautiful, like squirming flowers.

'Four.' Your cold, stained fingers roll the roach and stick it in your mouth. Four things you can hear. 'All that bloody banging. Fucking racket. And I can hear you!' You raise your voice, shouting at the door. 'Mumbling to yourself out there.' The cardboard roll falls from your lips and you scuffle to pick it up again, spilling tobacco into the refuse on the floor. Your boy mumbles a little, shifts in his sleep. He's exhausted after three days of watching you destroy yourself. Was it yesterday you remember him holding your hair back, wiping your mouth tenderly with the last clean dishtowel? Even just the memory of his brown eyes sends your vision into a crowded kaleidoscope of heart symbols. You pick up a wad of carpet mix, moist tobacco and batter crumbs and lint, and dump it in the middle of the paper.

'I can hear the crinkling of my coat and there's a siren outside somewhere. Three.' You stuff the roach back between your teeth and focus on trying to roll a real joint this time. Your hands haven't been steady since Slab left, but you never get any more used to it.

The paper crinkles, tears a little as you squeeze the filling into a cylinder and take the roach from your mouth to clumsily drop at one end. Three things you can smell.

'Sweat,' you say, raising your pathetic, crooked attempt to your lips. 'Pickle.' You lick the stripe and press the spliff shudderingly shut. 'Weed.'

It's a lie. You can't smell weed, or anything. The inside of your nostrils is burned ragged and caked in bitter, hot blankness.

'Two.' You delicately balance the spliff between your lips and pull your two lighters from your pockets, tip them together towards the end of the joint. One sparks, the other has fluid. They cannot function without each other, the perfect codependence. How a relationship should be, you think, and recognise that's unhealthy, born from desperation and too little sleep.

On the fifth attempt, the lighters ignite and you suck in hard, pulling the lit cherry up the paper until you're sure it's real.

Exhale. Cough. Two things you can feel.

'Smoke in my lungs.' You rock unsteadily to your feet and stagger to the window. It grinds open, the sashcord a thin, unpleasant grey from the years of sitting next to you on the windowsill while you puff. 'Cold.' The outside air hits your skin like a freezer burn, setting you to shivering and huddling in your coat.

Your boy shuffles, curls up tighter under Slab's great messy jacket. He's cold too. You resolve to make this a quick one. Better he's cold than inhaling this shit. You've done enough damage over the years without threatening him with all the photos on the tobacco pouches these days. Holes in chests, black lungs, vagina throats and the tinny screeching of mortuary trolleys are the stories the tobacco companies show to you to persuade you not to buy what they need you to buy.

You suck on the joint greedily, feeling your lungs expand past the throaty burn. 'One.' You exhale and pull a face like you did when you were a kid pretending to be a dragon. One thing you can taste. There is only one.

Your hand combs mindlessly through your pocket as you squint up at the clouds. Will it snow again today? Did it snow before? Two floors down, on the ground, there's grey slush piled up around wet, black tires and shiny, cold cars. It must have snowed.

The silence resounds. How long has it taken you to notice that the banging's stopped? You close your eyes into the screensaver behind your eyelids, a Mandelbrot set, and breathe slowly. No grumbling, no banging. No snoring. Whoever they were – whoever he was, because you're sure it was a he – they're gone now, walked away or died on your doorstep and really, would you even care if that was the case? As long as your boy didn't have to see it, would it really matter so much if someone who bangs on people's doors for hours in the middle of the night was to fall down and not get up again?

It's terrible, thinking like this. It makes you want to escape it, run out and away and leave yourself, your vile bits, behind.

You check your watch but it must be breaking. Five minutes since you last checked. But it doesn't show days. It must have been hours he was out there pounding away, and hours since he stopped. Your hands are shaking like a poet's first performance and rolling that spliff must have taken at least nine years.

You had plans yesterday, or tomorrow, whenever it was back before all this craziness fell out of you. Since the demons moved back in and took over in the form of little flat, plastic bags of white powder and crystals. Since you decided not to sleep.

It's not all bad though. The cold air's lively, dancing across your prickly, bumpy skin. It makes you feel lively too. Back before you went to see Slab again, paid him in money and sex and sharing whatever you bought, you had a plan. You were going to take your boy and leave. It was going to be one last night of fun, a long sleep and then out of the city, out into the world. You both have passports, you have a car. The world awaited you. But then the fog rolled in, and all of your hopes came crashing down and you did it again, let that last little stumbling block masquerade and parade itself around like it was a fortress wall, impregnable like you once thought you were, before that little pink plus sign showed up, smelling like urine and faded dreams.

You look in and see your boy, shivering now under Slab's coat, and your heart swells. No matter what else, you love him so much, so unutterably much, because he's beautiful and perfect and so, so special that really, it would be a shame to not wake him up and tell him so.

You stand up in a rush and graze your shoulder on the window, but even that feels good right now. Slamming the window down, you stumble over to the sofa and kneel beside it, flopping reverently forwards to cover your boy with your arms and your smell.

'Mum?' he asks, voice husky from too-ragged sleep. 'Are you ok?' Tears come to your eyes – he's always so considerate. You look up, eyes leaking and nose running green and white, and you smile into his eyes.

'I'm fine, my love, my darling, my butterfly. I'm so, so fine. Because I have you.' You clutch him tight, spasmodic. He wheezes out a compressed breath. 'Thank you, Ian. Thank you for being my kid. I love you so, so much. You know that? You do know that, don't you? I love you.'

'I know, Mum,' he says in his stoic, little-boy voice, and you release him a bit because you're not stupid, you know he can't breathe when you hold him like that, especially not when you're reeking of smoke.

'Today's the day,' you say, and you stand up. 'I'm going to take a shower. It's time, you knew that and I knew that and I'm so sorry I let you down the last few days but now, now we're really going.' You smile widely at him, but he just looks defeated, uncertain. Of course, he's tired, he hasn't slept well.

'It's ok littlee, you can sleep in the car. I'll sing to keep myself awake. Just get dressed and pack your things, we're going away.'

'Where are we going?' he asks, and maybe he's brightening up or maybe he's just playing along. Your brave little soldier. He's been let down so many times by you. But not this time. Today, you're really doing it.

'Amsterdam,' you say, because it's somewhere you've never been, and you're sure as hell not bringing anything with you on the ferry where the sniffer dogs could find it. You can get to Amsterdam in a day, maybe two, and stock up before going on to better places, more wild places. Places a boy can grow.

You turn and run into the bathroom, bouncing off the doorway on the way in like a pinball. You're being so clumsy, like your body's lost track of your mind. It's the cold.

The shower is scalding hot, about the only way to warm up in this fridge of a home. It turns your skin cherry-red and stinging, but even just the act of getting clean feels like God's forgiveness.

When you're out of the shower, you dry yourself roughly with the greasy towel like you're trying to rub life back into a dead limb, and start searching.

None of your clothes are clean, but some are less filthy than others. You haven't done laundry in weeks. But you've been organised. The passports, the vehicle documents, all of your boy's vaccination records, they're all together on the kitchen table where you knew you'd find them. You were so ready to go, but the time wasn't right. Now, it has come and you're going to go.

'Ian! Ian, are you ready?' the excitement in your voice tastes metallic, like blood and hysteria. You snort, and swallow. Backdrip, again. When will it end?

But none of that matters, not now you're leaving. Just you and your boy, crazy road warriors like in Mad Max, his favourite film.

You crash back into the living room with your little scuffed-up suitcase and the passports clutched triumphantly in one hand with your car keys.

He's sat on the sofa, still wrapped in Slab's big, smelly coat. His little fists pull it tight around him as you catch eyes. He hasn't lost that sad, brave, defeated look.

'Mum?' he asks, in that quiet, scared voice he uses far too often, and you hate that you make him speak like that.

'Yes, littlee.' You drop to your knees beside the sofa, and all the visuals and fractals in your eyes slow down, speed up, throb with your heartbeat.

'Mum, are you...' he looks you frankly in the eyes. 'Are you high right now?'

'No love, no, I'm just tired. I haven't slept all night, that's all. Once we're out of the city, first place we find I'll pull over and take a nap, yeah?' The words come out in a tumble, too eager to please and too fast.

'Mum, your eyes are all dark and you're holding me real tight like you do when you're on mandy.'

The word's like a stab in your heart, he's too young to know that, too young to have a mouthful of street slang for substances he should never have seen.

That last line, the one before the banging, the one that you found under the table leg. The one you thought was coke.

'It's ok, littlee,' you hear yourself saying. 'I want us to really do this this time. No more fucking up. We'll just get far enough that we know we're going, then I swear I'll pull over and sleep it off.'

He bites his lip and those big eyes frown, face crumpling like pain when he shakes his head. Your little boy stoic. 'No, Mum.' He reaches over and picks up the car keys where you dropped them on the sofa. 'You can't drive. I won't let you.'

For a brief moment, you're angry with this little boy who's like a crowbar, who can prise apart your hopes and dreams just by existing, just by speaking, but you're still rushing full of serotonin and you're so, so proud of him.

You look him in the eyes, your determined little soldier, and you see what he wants to say. *If you try to leave, or drive, or take me anywhere, I will call the police myself.* You know he thinks it, know he means it, know he won't. He loves you too much. Sometimes it's all you can do to stop yourself from falling at his feet and begging for absolution, for the peace of the confessional booth, for forgiveness. He's your ward and warden all in one, the only jailor of your heart, but he's not and never will be enough to stop you from craving.

You try one last time. 'I promise, Ian. I swear I'll sleep once we're out of town. I just need to get out of here, just enough to know we aren't coming back, and then I can stop lying to myself that we're leaving, because we really will be.'

He shakes his head and there are no tears, no words. Just that defeated, resigned look of the boy who's seen you fuck it up one too many times.

'Tomorrow,' you say. You take his face in your hands and make him look at you. The word tastes bitter on your tongue, like lying. 'Tomorrow, Ian. Tomorrow we're going. I promise.'

Later, when you've woken up from a deep nap, and your boy's still fast asleep, your fingers itch for your phone. You want to call someone, want to talk. You should probably tell Slab you're leaving town tomorrow. It's the neighbourly thing to do. You won't talk about drugs, or parties you'll be missing. Just... letting him know you're leaving. Like a real friend.

You press the green, scratched phone button, and it starts to ring.

GABRIEL OAKTHORN

Perchance to Dream

I REMEMBER THE DAY I died. It was quite sad, actually. One morning I woke up and I simply wasn't there. I'd never felt more alone.

I got up, nonetheless, went downstairs to make my morning cup of coffee, and sat and ate breakfast by myself. One bowl, one spoon, one portion of cornflakes. That, at least, was normal. I hadn't really eaten that much when I was alive. But I missed the companionable silence of having myself around. Now the silence was just... empty. The quiet of nobody around, rather than nobody talking.

The significance of being alone didn't escape me, of course. But right then I was a bit too shocked to really process it. To grieve, I guess. For a brief time I actually wondered if I'd gone out without telling myself. Ridiculous, right?

I called in sick, and went out anyway. If anyone recognised me they'd understand why I didn't feel up to working today. There was a sort of general understanding for that kind of thing back then.

Outside, the world was just starting to wake up, birds flitting from tree to tree and singing of love or something. People whose working day started half an hour after mine were visible in the slow lighting of windows in the street, clouds of steam erupting from bathroom vents.

The air was brisk, chill. I still had on my dressing gown. Somehow I'd thought far enough to discard my slippers and put on a pair of boots, even if they were wellingtons. I imagined the comedic figure I must cut, if anyone happened to glance out of their window and see me. It made me chuckle, and I turned to share it, forgetting I was alone.

The unfamiliar melancholy returned.

I walked on through the park, grateful for the wellingtons as I kicked up wet autumn leaves and left dark trails on the dewy grass. My feet would have been soaked in anything else – the hem of my dressing gown already was. I wasn't sure of where I was going, just that I needed to get there. Coddiwompling, you might say.

I spent at least half an hour sat on the swings in the playpark, swinging idly and listening to their melancholic creaking. They weren't really designed for someone of my weight. It didn't feel quite right without someone to push me, anyway.

The children were on their way to school by then, with their elders walking stoically beside them, seeing them safely to the classroom. Some of them stared at me curiously or fearfully. I waved, but all but one little girl looked away. I understood why.

It's unnerving seeing young people out alone in playparks, particularly if they're wearing dressing gowns and wellingtons at eight in the morning. I guessed I probably looked like a drunk or drug addict. If they had come close enough, though, my breath would have smelled of coffee rather than booze, harsh reality rather than fantasy and dreams.

I looked across the park to see four people walking a dog. The younger two, about my age, were arm in arm and laughing about something while the older couple eyed each other with awkward weariness and a kind of regretful patience. Sometimes I envy that funny alloromantic lot, those who engage in that seemingly worldwide search for romance and sexual partnership. But then I think about how much easier it is to fit two people in an apartment built for one than it is to fit four, and I'm glad I'm me. My life has been made significantly easier by my lack of interest in that arena.

That morning it would have been nice though, to have had someone to wake up next to, someone who'd *know*.

But it didn't happen that way. So it goes.

The next day, of course, I couldn't delay going into work any longer, so I showed up. My coworkers were very kind, in that hushed way that people are when death comes calling. Told me they were sorry for my loss, was I sure I was feeling up to working, was there anything they could do for me? It was all very sweet but really it set my teeth on edge. One can only experience so many shocked expressions and unnecessary apologies in a single day before starting to lose one's grip.

The following days were much the same, though by that point I'd started to severely notice the differences between myself and everyone else. I started to count ten co-workers instead of five, two customers instead of one. I paid closer attention to my regulars and the ways they'd changed. One of them came in three days in a row and every time she looked different. One morning, a long-broken nose and missing a few back teeth; the next a sad, forlorn look but a warm, full smile. On the third day she was dead, too. We didn't see her for a couple of days and I felt a few brief pangs of sympathy. Empathy, even. Maybe I was even slightly relieved I wasn't alone, as unattractive as that is.

Several days later she came back in and she was alive again. I stared at her. The broken nose was back, this time on both of her.

'How did you do it?' I whispered as I handed over her usual black coffee with vanilla.

She grinned broadly despite her two black eyes, and I saw those back teeth, two missing. 'You remembered!'

I didn't know if she meant the coffee order or that she'd been dead yesterday.

Her smile dropped and she leaned in close. I leaned in too.

'I left him,' she whispered. 'Couldn't stay, could I, after seeing that?' She shuddered. 'I keep going back but that was it. I can't let him kill me. As soon as I decided, for real, I came back to myself. Knew he'd try to do it anyway from the look of me, but really I guess what's a broken nose and some teeth missing compared with missing all of me?' She gave me a sympathetic look and a worried smile. She felt somehow tenuous, liminal. She wanted to go back. But she couldn't. It's so much harder to betray yourself when you see the living proof of it right in front of your eyes.

'Maybe you'll get yourself back too?' she suggested before moving away. Her elder self walked close behind her, that crooked, healed nose almost pressed to her neck. She would not let her go back.

I worked in a haze for the rest of the day. I had not known, never been told. Why weren't we told this? Once your elder was gone, that was it. You had a use-by date. A 'best before'.

When I clocked out, I wandered aimlessly. My life as it was would kill me. Or I'd die of some disease. I tried desperately to remember what I'd looked like the day before I died. My face slipped from my mind, hovered just out of reach. Had I been thin? Fat? Had I had a purple nose and bloated pouches under my eyes? Did I look stressed? Sad? Peaceful?

I found myself back at that playpark and sat on the swings again, ignoring the children squawking around me on the climbing frames.

I had been thin, I decided, but soft. Lacking in tone. I had had clear skin, free of makeup or blemishes. Long hair, tied back, and grey clothes. I had looked... not peaceful. Bored. Tired out, worn thin. I wish I had thought to ask myself if I still worked at the same café, pouring the same drinks, received a nod or a shake of the head in return. But it was too late now. All those words, left unsaid. All that silent communication missed. I should have listened to that silence more.

Something had to change.

The next day I called in sick again. It was a difficult time, I could get away with it. I sat on my one chair in my kitchen and drank a hot chocolate. I didn't usually, but what harm could it do me now?

What did I want? I asked myself. What had I wanted back before I fell into drudgery and boredom and notice periods and rent payments and keeping bread on the table?

I had wanted something bigger. Something exciting. I had wanted something. What did I want now? The answer, which came quickly, was surprisingly easy. I wanted to be braver.

Being careful had not given me my long life. In fact, I had died relatively young. So what was stopping me?

I didn't wait. Within an hour I was in town, at a walk-in appointment at a barber's.

'Cut it all off,' I told them.

'You sure?' he asked teasingly. 'All of it?'

'All of it,' I confirmed.

I left with my old hair in a plastic bag, all two feet of it. What was I going to do with it? Who knew? It was mine! In all honesty I later donated it to a wigmaking program. What did I need it for? But that didn't come until later.

I went out to a bar and drank some ridiculous cocktail with three names and a sparkler in it.

'Celebrating something?' the bartender asked me warily, eyeing the empty space beside me where I should have been.

'Yes,' I replied, and drank.

I came up with a list of new rules:

1. Fear no danger. If your destiny cannot change, you have nothing to lose. You cannot die before your use by date.
2. If your destiny can change, greet yourself warmly wherever you are when you meet again.
3. No more rules

It seemed so simple, and in a way it was. I carefully calculated my finances (old habits die hard), and I worked out that I had enough money to buy a return plane ticket anywhere in the world, if I took a budget airline.

Then I went one step further and took it all out in cash. I was still courteous, so I called work to let them know I quit. They were understandably shocked but I steeled myself and refused to go in to work my notice. They let me take it as holiday. Another week's wages. That was good. Even with my new rules, I wanted emergency backup.

I illegally sublet my flat for the rest of my contract and handed the keys over two days later. It had come furnished, I owned nothing but my clothes, knickknacks and pot plants.

The plants I gave to the new tenant as a gift, the knickknacks I put in a charity shop, except a handful of particularly precious ones who either came with me or got buried beneath a tree in the park in a watertight box. I had no family to leave them with, you see. None I was willing to visit, anyway.

I winnowed my clothes down to one backpack and put the rest in a clothes deposit bin. The man in the shop was very perturbed to see me rifling through my big suitcase to see what I could fit in the backpack he had just sold me.

Then I was ready. Despite travelling so rarely, I had kept my passport in date. I walked to the edge of town, toward the airport, and stopped halfway up the slip road to the motorway. I stuck out my thumb.

The wait was agonising. I questioned my sanity, my intelligence, my trust in strangers. I tested my own patience far more than the stream of cars that didn't pull over. I waved and smiled. It took forever. Then a blue car – I will always remember this – saw me, slammed on its brakes and pulled into the layby. A friendly face looked out.

'Where you going?'

'Dover,' I replied.

'Hop in.'

After that it was easier. I knew to trust that someone would stop. Even on bare roads with no one for miles in either direction, someone would drive past and stop eventually. It was easier, perhaps, because there was only one of me. Usually one would need at least two spare seats for a hitchhiker, but I was compact, alone. Perhaps it made people more kindly toward me too. I grew used to it, the waiting and the boredom and the ache in my arms. The exultation when a car slowed. I trusted everyone and everyone, it seemed, trusted me. Well, almost everyone. There were a few hairy moments, but they were vastly outweighed by the kindness of most of the strangers I met.

I travelled a long way. After a touristic stint around western Europe, I hitchhiked my way east and south, through the Mediterranean, Greece, Turkey. I loved Istanbul. Finally I was spat out of a lorry on the far side, in Asia. It didn't look much different from the countries I had just left, really.

I felt more nervous there, for a short while. I don't know why. Racist fearmongering back home, I guess. But Asia was kind to me, as Europe had been. I headed east, down through Iran, Afghanistan, Pakistan. India was magnificent. I climbed mountains, different from the ones where I'd learned to snowboard in France, and learned to dance by the south sea. I was amused by how much 'travel', to other travellers, seemed to include sex. As if they could taste a hundred different varieties of it in a hundred different countries, even though they primarily only had sex with each other. I ignored it entirely. Friends found me, travelled alongside me for a while here and there. It was humbling and delightful to realise I was not alone, not the only one circumnavigating the globe on their thumb.

But easier alone. After all, everyone else came in pairs. Or most of them. Those who were like me, just young and nothing else, solitary figures, stayed with me longer. We understood.

I no longer wore grey, except for the dust. My hair was short and messily cut and I wore bracelets, and ankle strings. My clothing was a riot of colour, tangled up in a bright mess. I had tattoos, and a nose piercing. In the mirror, I was someone else. But still I was alone.

I was very happy. Sometimes it didn't even register how lonely I was, without myself standing stoically by my side. I began to believe I would never find myself again. That my destiny could not change.

I went across the sea to Australia and New Zealand, determined to be braver still. I went skiing, snowboarding, rock climbing. I learned to surf. SCUBA entered my life and I swam with sharks and jellyfish, daring their tendrils to come close. I bungee jumped and dove off cliffs and rode a giant trapeze swing across a canyon. Nothing killed me. In death, I had become more alive than I had ever been.

I made my peace with it. Perhaps my destiny could have changed, but I had gone about it the wrong way. Maybe I had never had a chance. But I wouldn't change it. I had lived more since I died than in all the years of my life before that. If my time was going to be up sooner than others, what of it? At least I'd had fun.

I fell into the habit of meditating every day, and stretching out my tired body and tight shoulders. I returned to India. The Americas called, but I wasn't ready for them yet. I compromised and returned to Europe, finally reaching the sea. I settled on Tenerife for half a year, slowing down at last. My body thanked me for it. Friends gathered around me. I had never known I was likeable before I died. One night I was invited to some party celebrating the full moon, and for once I said yes.

Music pulsed gently out into the night from the cave where it roared loud and the bass rolled through my stomach. I sat on the cliff and looked out over the sea, where the moonlight shimmered on the water. I did not feel so alone anymore.

Somehow over the years I had become used to the fact that where everyone else had four feet, two heads, two pairs of hands for dancing and holding, I was complete within one body. I wondered briefly where I would go, what I would do next, but it didn't matter. I would do something. It would come in its time.

Someone settled on the rock beside me and sat silently watching the moon. It arced high above us, its face resplendent and glowing. I was grateful it was a clear night. The water rippled gently below, waves coming in to the shore and sucking back out before returning.

The quiet endured. If a silence can feel familiar, different, that one did. It stretched thick and warm between us like an old blanket we pulled around our shoulders, the way I used to feel when it was just the two of me, alone in my flat. It felt like home.

I looked up.

The Escape Clause

HELLO, AND WELCOME to Afterlife Insurance, here to meet all of your post-mortem needs. Yes, yes, that's it, sitting up already, well done! May I just say, most of the recently deceased take at least five minutes to regain that sort of posture – you're already off to a fighting start. Here, let me – getting one's feet on the clouds for the first time can be a hell of a task, if you'll pardon the pun.

There we go, upright already, just fine and dandy, fine and dandy. And may I congratulate you on your decision to take out an afterlife insurance policy with us? It really doesn't do to leave these things up to fate, does it?

How was your death? Pleasant, I hope? Well I suppose that's one way to go out with a bang, eh your honour? There are worse ways. So very many worse ways.

Now, how's your memory? No early-onset dementia? Brain damage? Fantastic. It can take a while to even yourself out after those. Can you remember much prior to your arrival here? No? Well not to worry, not to worry. It will all come flooding back in a few moments, I'm sure. Coffee? I'm afraid the beans are a bit out of date, but it's better than nothing, I always say.

Oh someone's in a bad mood, look at this mess. Beans bloody everywhere. Oh well, not to worry, we all have our good days and bed days don't we your honour? Should have seen Raph this morning, he was on the line to Beelzebub's lawyers all morning. Bound to wear anyone ragged.

Here we go, black coffee. Sugar? I take as much of it as I can get these days. Righto, let's go in my office.

That's it, bit quieter in here. Do have a seat while I dig out your file. Crikey, that's a colourful life you had there isn't it? Awful lot of highlighter. Oh don't worry about that. They colour code it you see – pink for deadly sins, green for the little everyday mishaps and yellow for good deeds. Why yellow? I have no idea. Good as gold, I presume. Yes there is a lot of green, but that's no problem really. Green is always included in the standard policy. Acquittals all around. No real need for a trial, it all becomes a bit of a waste of time really. Still, good to clear the air, eh your honour?

Right, so let's see what we have here then. Drug abuse, fornication, tattoos... My goodness you ate a lot of bacon, didn't you? The usual really, all that's old hat.

No, most of your early life's quite expected really, your honour. They've stapled some of the pages, though, that's never a good sign. You enjoy your coffee, I'll just have a proper flick through.

Oh. Oh, I see. Hmm. Yes, well, we may possibly have the teensiest of weensiest little hiccups here, you see. The thing is, your honour, we... well, we *saw* you sign that deal with the Devil. No, no, I assure you, it's in your file, and these things are all done automatically these days. Helps with the understaffing issues – done ourselves out a job, you see, what with all our most promising candidates getting savvy enough to take out one of our policies before they're unlucky enough to wind up here. Oh no, your honour, I *love* my job, really. Wouldn't be anywhere else.

Ah yes, back to your previously-mentioned *contract*... Well, the problem is, you see, we have it on file that you absolutely, positively signed this contract, and you were sober when you did so. See, we would have some leeway if you'd been intoxicated – informed consent being what it is and all that.

No, no I assure you, you *did*, but who can blame you if it's slipped your mind? It's not the sort of encounter you'd want to remember, by any means. I'd give a golden goose to forget the last time I met Lucifer, the smarmy bastard.

Evidence? Your honour, these files aren't made up willy-nilly, they're full and complete records of your entire life.

Well, I mean, we *could* check the tapes if you really want to go to all that trouble? You do? You're sure? Alrighty then, let me just find your disc, it'll be in this folder somewhere... Yes, I'm afraid we're hideously behind the times – budgets only stretch so far, unfortunately.

If you'd be so kind as to close your eyes. And... here we go. That? That's the placenta, your honour. Oh yes, that's you as a toddler – adorable, isn't it? It's such a treat, really, to go through the whole thing like this, in fast-forward – gives one such perspective.

Oh, don't worry about that, that's the sort of sin we can sort out with our hands nailed down, your honour. No, that's not the issue at all. Or that one – I mean, who hasn't committed something similar at least fifty times, am I right? Minor infractions, all of them. Even the 10 Commandments are a bit iffy these days – who do you know who *doesn't* take the Lord's name in vain? No, I was mostly joking about the bacon - vegetarianism is categorically not a requirement with us around, it just gets you into Brahma's good books. Useful place to be if you ask me, but a lifetime without meat is not a lifetime worth having, I always say. Anyway, all of that 'rules' shebang is highly overrated. That's what we're here for.

Oh goodness me, I got distracted, where are we now? Say, this section's quite dark, isn't it? Cocaine addiction, you say? Bloody awful stuff, never touch it myself. Ah look, there you go – rehab and all. Lovely. Folks had something set aside, did they? Sensible, especially with musicians about. And... there it is. September 2011, the day before you packed up from the facility and went home. Your readings show your system's as clean as a whistle right there, and if I'm not wrong, this is the crucial scene. Let's relive this one at life speed. Slowing down, slowing down... And there we go.

So there's your doctor, you remember her, I'm sure, running you through her checklist – I hate bloody checklists with a passion, don't you – and signing you off. There, I'm sure that must be in some ways quite a good memory. The day you were officially recognised as clean and got to go home, free as a bird.

Now, there's the bugger. See that one coming through the door, with the clipboard? Yes, the blonde one. Well of course he's pretty, he's Lucifer. Now, see there – he hands you the documents on the clipboard, and the pen? It's fancy, isn't it, he always was a show-off. Now this is the bit that's... well, I don't want to say a snag, per se, but you know what I mean. You read it, you see. From end to end, even the small print. And you sign it.

The thing is, we specifically do not offer cover against contracts with Lucifer, and your policy with us does state that quite clearly. It would be uneconomical in the extreme for us to offer him a soul for every Faust he recruits – we'd soon be out of stock. Now, on the other hand we can try to fight it in court, but Mephistopheles will have all his legal team looking at this too, and it's going to be very hard to argue that you were in any way of unsound mind when you signed this, given that your doctor had signed you off as clearheaded less than two minutes prior.

Your honour, you're a fabulously wealthy, internationally-acclaimed musician with a resounding immunity to substance abuse; I don't think there's any way we can argue he didn't uphold his part of the deal.

Of course we have our own legal team, your honour. They've already read through it forwards, backwards, sideways and upside down. Lucifer's contracts are watertight these days, beyond the obvious.

Your honour, have you read Dr Faustus? Look, I know it's old, but it's a classic – was even before my time. No you really don't want to know how long I've been working here, your honour. See, Dr Faustus didn't feel able or willing or deserving, or what-have-you, to ask for God's forgiveness before he was taken. If he had done so, the contract would have been nullified – all those years of love and riches and fame for free.

No, I'm afraid the escape clause isn't valid post-mortem, your honour. Your death is considered the fulfilment of the contract. Even if it wasn't, you can't just say 'I'm sorry, Yahweh', you have to actually *repent*. That means you have to genuinely feel guilty, feel sorry and be determined to change your ways. It's quite a tall order for a deathbed, that's why so many sinners end up locked out of the pearly gates no matter what the good gods have told them.

No, the gates aren't real. Or they are. It depends on who's looking. I don't see it, personally.

Anyway, right now, your main issue is this impending legal disaster. I'm afraid in cases like these it's very rare to get a plea deal. And by rare I mean we have a zero percent track record.

No, we don't offer legal advice as standard during our clients' lifetimes. Because we simply don't have the resources for it, your honour. No matter how much time we have available, we are, as I say, severely understaffed and we have over half a billion customers on this planet alone.

Ha, if I had a pardon for every time someone asked me that question. No, I'm sorry your honour, I don't mean to make light. Still, it's good to keep upbeat. Sometimes a chuckle's all that'll get you through the day, isn't that right your honour? Laughter is the best medicine they say.

So, back to the main point. Your honour, I'll be frank. Under these circumstances it is simply impossible for us to enter into an expensive legal battle that is guaranteed to lose. Not to mention your policy is void. I'm terribly sorry, but you haven't got a leg to stand on. Now now your honour, that won't do. We have a strict policy against abuse in this establishment and we don't stand for that sort of thing. Yes, well. It's only eternity. You'll get used to it in a few centuries. Possibly. It's a good idea to try to develop a Zen mindset – acceptance is the first part of letting go, after all. No, I'm even that won't help you to reverse the decisions you made in life. You simply cannot escape fate, your honour, it's just common sense. And several hundred years of experience. Take it from me, you don't have a snowball's chance.

Why not? Because, your honour, you are an unmitigated sinner. Look at the receipts! You embezzled, you drank, you quite frankly wrecked yourself on drugs, you fornicated, you got divorced four times and deliberately ensured that your partners would receive nothing, I mean my goodness you even took a policy out with us! And even if we could get you off for all that, you had to go one further, didn't you? You signed a watertight, legally binding – *spiritually* binding – contract with *Lucifer* of all people. I mean, why would you even bother taking out an After-life policy after all that? Quite frankly, your honour, it was a waste of money and I put my hands up. There is nothing we can do. You've done yourself out of Heaven.

Your best bet is to start doing some mental and spiritual preparation, your honour. I can only drag this meeting out for so long before Beelzebub starts knocking on the door. It's astounding he's been polite enough to wait this long. Must be feeling merciful – giving you some time to process. Yes, devils can be exceedingly polite *and* merciful, thank you.

Look, my friend, I have a lot of sympathy. Empathy, even. God knows we've all been sat where you are now, and I know it's an uncomfortable place. Think I even sat in that very chair back in my day. Not very comfy, is it? I applied for funding for a new one a century or so back, but they wouldn't grant it. Always the way with higher ups, isn't it, they never care so much about the customers as their bottom line.

Ah, I think that's Beelzebub now. Well my friend, it's been an honour. I wish you all the luck in the world, though admittedly it won't do you much good.

Yes, Beelz, we're coming. Don't get your tail in a twist.

Righto your honour, we'd best get you moving. Doesn't do to keep them waiting, see. Alrighty, there we go. Well done, you really are getting the hang of those motor functions aren't you?

We're coming, Beelz!

Right then your honour, deep breath now together, that's it. And on three. One, two, three.

Hello Beelzebub, sorry to keep you waiting. Now your honour, if you'd care to follow my friend Beelzebub here, he'll show you to your final resting place. It's been a privilege, your honour. And don't forget, it's only eternity!

GENRE-FLUID

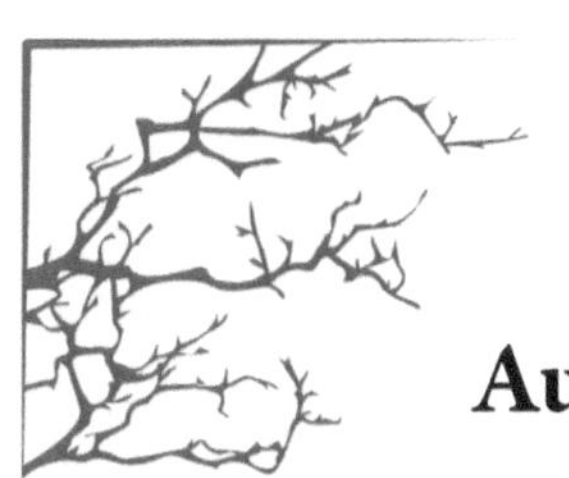

Author's Note

I PUT THIS COLLECTION together for my grandmothers, whom I am very lucky to have.

Thank you so much Granny Jo and Granny Hilary. You have both been such important key players in my life, and I am so grateful that you are my grandmothers. Thank you for all of your support and love and nurturing over the years, and for creating so many happy, silly, fun, exciting and loving memories for all of your grandchildren, shared or individual. I love you both very much!

Don't miss out!

Visit the website below and you can sign up to receive emails whenever Gabriel Oakthorn publishes a new book. There's no charge and no obligation.

https://books2read.com/r/B-A-HEQM-LPAKB

BOOKS2READ

Connecting independent readers to independent writers.

About the Author

Gabriel Oakthorn (they/them) specialises in fiercely tender revolution, radical honesty and finding divinity in the monstrous. They're a Purbeck Valley slam champion and Hammer and Tongue veteran, and have been crowned the 'monarch of the extended metaphor'.

Their Bedtime Stories can be found on the Lucid Tales YouTube channel, and their short story collection, 'genre-fluid' is available from all major ebook sellers. Other works have been published by Dorset Magazine, Wordmakers Press, Cream Scene Carnival and Nebulous Magazine, among many others.

Photo by @2d_photography_uk

Read more at https://www.linktree.com/lucideers.

About the Publisher

Lucid Tales is a loose collective of tellers of tall tales and weavers of ragged myth. They perform across the UK and beyond, and publish revolutionary books inspired by mythology, folklore and faerietale.

Read more at https://www.linktree.com/lucideers.